What w. ..... demon was tearing down the canyon toward us with the speed of a locomotive. It must have been a giant for I heard the snapping and twisting of tree trunks shattered at its very passage and I wondered aloud how we could possibly fight this devil.

Rockwell shouted there was no fighting it.

I did not understand what could cause him fear and now as a leviathan was thundering toward us he swiftly moved to the upper ledge and grabbed a secure hold of a boulder. I shouted at him over the approaching din, that perhaps no bullet or blade could harm him but what was I to do against this new foe and what was it?

Then the mowing demon, formed of crunching twisted roots, brambles and tree branches' turning end over end pushed by deep brown waters came rushing into view. Scraping hands of wood and water pawed at us, spit in our faces and took hold with malevolent abandon.

One of the Paiute braves was pierced through the gut and carried away into the morass, churned, chewed and swallowed before he could even scream.

— **Right Hand Man**

Whispers Out Of The Dust

A Haunted Journey Through The Lost American West

David J. West

LOST REALMS PRESS

For Athena

CONTENTS

Foreword:..2

The Toad in My Study 5

Jornada del Muerte 12

Stranger Come Knocking.......................................24

Curse of the Lost City...27

Skullduggery..36

The Big Mouth..42

Gods of the Old Land..48

Right Hand Man 60

The Thing in the Root Cellar...............................95

Black Jack's Last Ride 108

A Rose for Miss Dolly...116

If I Call to the Pit..120

Devil Takes the Hindmost...................................128

The Groaning Desk..133

The Blessing Way...139

Chief John Rides Again...154

Wisp of a Thing..158

There was a Woman Dwelt by a Graveyard............160

Bury Me Deep..166

Return of the Toad 182

Afterword:..185

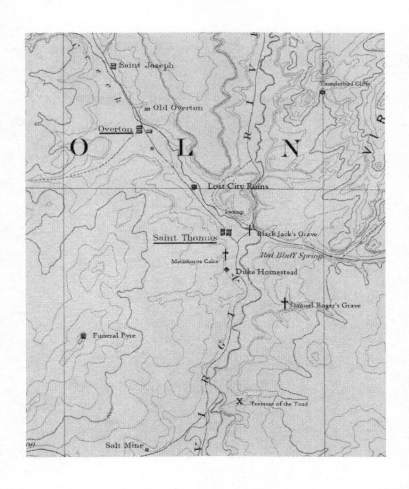

Map of Saint Thomas and thereabouts

"And thou shall be brought down, and shall speak out of the ground, and thy speech shall be low out of the dust, and thy voice shall be, as of one that hath a familiar spirit, *out of the ground, and thy speech shall whisper out of the dust."*

— Isaiah 29: 4

"Go west, young man." — Horace Greely

Foreword:

Have you ever heard of St. Thomas? Probably not. This book began as an interesting collection of journals, articles and newspaper clippings relating to that ghost town. It would be difficult to find a more barren and lost land that yet had some small amount of moisture present than St. Thomas. For the last seventy five odd years the town itself was drowned under sixty feet of tap water for Las Vegas via Hoover Dam.

St. Thomas was a literal hotbed of haunted happenings. A veritable Mecca of the outlandish and horrific all contained within the Moapa valley. And for the sake of a fascinating story I will face and pray in that cursed direction five times a day, My Friend.

Founded in January of 1865 by Mormon settlers sent by Brigham Young to grow cotton. St. Thomas rests at the conflux of the Muddy and Virgin Rivers not far from the Colorado which feeds that leviathan Lake Mead. At most there were only ever 600 souls in the city upon founding (usually less). The initial settlers remained thereabouts for only just over six years. Others moved in and out over the course of the next sixty years.

While all other documentable sources indicate a problem with federal taxes and the filling of the reservoir as a reason for their departure, other possibilities presented themselves as I read on. I have no reason to doubt the veracity of the parochial testimonies claimed herein. At every turn in my research their tale is backed up by cold hard facts.

To both the seeker and the curious, a warning:

I have only edited pertinent content so as to get to the raw-head and bloody bones of this collection of tales. Spelling and grammar errors have remained untouched so as not to pollute the journalistic integrity nor stain the intent of any of the numerous and possibly fallible witness statements.

I have also taken the liberty of placing chapter titles, quotes and footnotes where none previously existed. I cannot resist an overly dramatic chapter title. You, Reader, should have the privilege to taste the copper in the air, smell the lingering brimstone and feel the cold caress of a spiders legs upon your bare skin. The pulp fiction heart in me is still very much alive despite this black pilgrimage into the wilds of academia and non-fiction. My wanderings herein lean toward storyteller and grim chronicler rather than documentarian or, heaven forbid, "respectable writer".

The title quote from Isaiah is apropos considering the God-fearing nature of most of these observers. By and large they were all (whether Saint or Sinner) people who knew on which side of the pearly gates they stood.

Everything contained herein is absolutely true at least so much as the chroniclers of these found documents understood it. I suspect most of them never believed that this material would be shared with anyone outside of possible family members or law enforcement. In the case of one of these journals, there was even an active attempt at suppression!

But I digress . . .

If indeed there are any other misspellings or missteps or even misdeeds—they are my own. I would suggest you praise or complain to me alone for any misgivings contained herein and take care to not harass the dead for their hasty words or tragic failings. They've already done their time and toil here on earth and you don't want to be inviting any of them back.

David J. West
Lehi, Utah
August 22, 2015

" — A country in ruins, dissolved by the peltings of the storms of ages, or turned inside out, upside down, by terrible convulsions in some former age . . . Poor and worthless as was the country, it seemed everywhere strewn with broken pottery, well glazed, and striped with unfading colors."

— Parley P. Pratt 1849

The Toad in My Study

Or How I Found these Mysteries

At first glance I believed this found documents had belonged to some wishful armchair treasure hunter desperate to find a gold nugget that would solve his problems. I would have soon thrown it all out but something crawled out at me from the waste basket of ages, croaking, 'Here I Am, Come and See'.

Digging in and spending quite a few dark nights and early mornings making sense of the twisted thing, I was presented with a much more sinister portrait than initially imagined. This was not the work of a single collector, even a deranged one. This, My Friend, was the trial all antiquarians such as myself, dream of receiving.

That this work became much larger than first expected is an understatement of rude proportions. Originally this was to be only an interesting historical blog post about what I had discovered. I thought perhaps I would share the story via the usual social media avenues. But rather than this being like so much of my fiction which often enough the tale grows in the telling, this rather revealed itself to have far more material and macabre repercussions for those involved, albeit luckily not myself included yet.

Now, as to the discovery of the collection: Some may know that I am a literary pulp-fiction writer and therefore love books a bit more than usual person. My large and handsome library/study houses some seven thousand volumes. I still frequently haunt both new and used book stores on the lookout for another interesting acquisition. As I suspect a great many writers are, I am drawn to the curious, historical and dramatic.

I enjoy new books from varied names and authors, both friend and foe. I am drawn, however, to dusty back corners of used shops where shelves straining under the weight of nearly forgotten tomes, books that were abandoned to the dark recesses and printed long before I was born.

Strangely enough this particular collection of writings did not begin in such a darkened place but in the overly bright sunshine of a Deseret Industries‖. I happened to be in Las Vegas. And as is my usual habit, I went searching for old rare books that, more often than not, the employees have no idea on the value thereof.

Disheartened at a lack of interesting books, I settled on a few large picture frames. As I drove around back to have them loaded, I heard a young employee complain about a truckload of materials. They had just been dropped off unceremoniously without the delivery person so much as waiting for a tax receipt. Having once worked in a similar establishment I can vouch that when a parent or elder family

---

‖ Deseret Industries is a thrift store franchise maintained throughout the Mormon-centric west for those who are unfamiliar. There are over forty such thrift stores spread out mostly over Utah, along with some in Idaho, Nevada, Washington, Arizona and California.

member passes on, the family, having no interest or care for their departed members possessions, dumps them en-masse at a local thrift store. Often what is worthless junk to one person is a priceless treasure to another. Antiques Roadshow anyone?

In particular, there was a large heavy trunk that had just been dropped off. The tattooed young men questioned each other on what to do with it. It was a faded blue steel with copper accents. This one was much water damaged and in poor shape.

The young man complained to his fellow temporarily employed comrade that he could not lift it on his own. They then attempted to throw it in the dumpster beside my car but even together they could not lift it the gargantuan monstrosity. They looked to me hopefully.

Instead of assisting I suggested they open it, remove the materials inside, make it lighter and do the job themselves. They, however gifted, did not know how to open it. I showed them being familiar with the old practice of latches and snaps.

Inside amidst the stink of mothballs and mildew was quite a collection of moldering newspapers, rotten old books, shoes and a leather satchel. 'It's all junk', declared the younger of the two employees. Not disagreeing with him, the other prepared to pick up the debris and toss it overhand into the dumpster.

Knowing that neither would care nor object, I rifled along with them to sate my own curiosity and see what else was inside the trunk. Picking up the leather satchel, I was struck with the weight of it. I placed it on the ground beside me to see what was beneath it. There were a few more old newspapers and yellowed parchments of illegible handwritten notes. The water damage was pervasive.

Though I had hoped to see something truly worthwhile, alas there was not.

After disposing of numerous items, the two employees hefted the entire trunk and tossed it into the dumpster. They then proceeded to walk back into the yard area unconcerned for the lonely satchel that remained at my feet. I had not been impressed with the sour leather bag, though its weight did cause some curiosity. I waited a moment until the employees were out of sight and drew back the tight straps and peered inside, half expecting dead mice.

Instead, the satchel was full of stacked papers, some yellowed and hand written and oddly legible considering the rest of the trunk. Others appeared to be newspaper clippings or magazine pages torn from whatever article was of interest to the former owner. There was also a small stone statue that looked like a crudely carved toad made from reddish desert stone. This was enough to capture me. Regardless of the foul musty odor permeating from the bag, I put it in my trunk and drove away.

I forgot about the bag for another week while sightseeing, casino work and such. It was not until I was home that I remembered the odorous bag which I put in storage so as not to befoul my study.

Now weeks later, I was looking for a particular volume that had not found its way into the study, and smelled the bag. Planning to look inside once more then throw it away, I opened it and drew forth the toad-like idol along with the stack of papers. Thoroughly searching the bag until it was empty, I threw it in the trash. Then I looked through the papers while thinking the toad might make an interesting conversational paperweight.

The collection of papers appeared random until I was struck by the oldest of them. It was from a Spanish conquistador in 1540 and translated to English in January of 1865. The most recent of the collection was dated August of 1938. The journals were from a variety of different people. Only some few items were newspaper and or magazine clippings relating to the actual stories at hand.

And now I shall begin to put the story together in as readable and linear fashion as possible. I will interject some footnoted report of items and articles I found to substantiate the unfolding chronicle.

The stone toad now sits upon my desk staring blankly as I type and I wonder to myself, "Does it approve?"

WHISPERS OUT OF THE DUST — DAVID J. WEST

"Good countries are not for us..."

— George Q. Cannon

In January of 1865 Mormon pioneers struggled into the Moapa Valley and created the first settlement of *our* age there in St. Thomas. As they set to making the land blossom as the desert rose for themselves they did on occasion discover some strange relics of a bygone era.

The valley, of course, had been inhabited for some time previously by the Paiutes and the Anasazi before them, but with no known written record from them, our story begins with the savage tale left by the first deranged Europeans to have visited the valley. Rather than bog this narrative down anymore I leave you with the curious find of one Elias McGinnies.

The original blue bottle containing the words of Diego Matamoros

"Granted that they did not find the riches of which they had been told; they did find the next best thing—a place in which to search for them."

— Pedro de Castenada[2]

Jornada del Muerte

Statement of Elias McGinnies: January 1865

Prior to finding the blue bottle, I drew lots with the other settlers for my demarcation of property and they were indeed fair with me despite not being of their faith[3]. I did receive a substantial amount of acreage on the western edge of the settlements and will gain an agreed allotment of water once the canal is finished.

As I was clearing my fields of stone, I did speed the plow over a particularly large gathering of loose rock. It seemed out of place and purposeful in its placement. As I carried the stones out to the edge of my field I found broken human bones and deteriorating rags beneath them. I soon found two full skeletons and could tell that they were not Indian remains but Spaniards. They had no wealth, weapons or tools to speak of, though piles of rust did permeate the dig. The one artifact I could find among them was a small rotting wooden chest that contained only a small blue bottle corked with some few fragile papers rolled up inside. The following

---

[2] Pedro de Castenada was the historian and chronicler for Coronado.
[3] Elias McGinnies was the only non-Mormon in the original party of settlers of St. Thomas. He presumably got along very well with them.

written by a lost conquistador name of Diego
. I imagine he would appreciate that his story was
found though I am not. Translating it to the best of my ability
is a hair raising episode indeed. I do have some questions in
places I did not understand, perhaps someday I will get the
answer to these terrible mysteries. Until then I sleep with my
hand on my gun and my door locked. I have urged my
neighbors to do the same so long as we remain in this valley.

From the pen of Diego de la Vega Matamoros: 1540

I have but a few scraps of paper with which to record my
last days. To whomever finds this record, caution, these are
dangerous lands and perilous times. Keep wary for both they
that cry out in the sky and also the whisperers in the dark
that each lie in wait upon this Journey of Death.

I have done many bloody things in my life. I did the
savage work of the Inquisition serving faithfully under Diego
Deza carrying on in the footsteps of Torquemada. The
atrocities at my hand were unnumbered in Spain alone. And
then I did come to the New World and did serve another
madman Hernan Cortez who rewarded my service of blood
for it was I who slew the Aztec giant Tzilacatzin[†]! Me, Diego
Matamoros! And though I am older yet I volunteered to go
with Coronado and conquer new lands by the strength of my
sword arm. And thus do I come to my end, reaping what
horror I have always sown.

This is how I met my death.

Having escaped from the murderous tribe of Indians that
enslaved us for the last three months, my companions,

[†] Legendary giant Aztec defender of Tenochtitlan known for throwing
stones and killing Spaniards.

Francisco de la Vaca, Juan Castillo, Don Hernandez and myself were forced to flee up the El Rio de Buena Guia[†]? We managed to take back the most meager of supplies in our flight including our boots, blankets, several saddle bags, these few papers, a canteen, a single blue bottle from Cordoba but alas no weapons. We were cut off in our escape at every turn and found it impossible to return to our comrades downriver who must surely believe that we are dead by now and as I write this, I am sure that our end will soon come to pass.

I have not slept in many days and grow weary as my eyes see things that my mind says cannot exist. I have heard naked drums in the forbidden empty desert and seen caravans of ghosts on some grand precession into the next world, only casually strutting through ours for a short time before disappearing back into the void of sand.

It is troubling as we have experienced these things that cannot be and yet oft times one will see or hear what the others cannot.

We had plenty of water as we moved upstream but when the Indians flanked and cut us off we had to head into the Empty Quarter to evade them.

Our salvation was a double-edged sword in that the treacherous Indians would not follow us to that cursed realm. They ceased to pursue us beyond the river's edge and we wondered if it was but a ruse, then as we attained some higher ground we could see that they would not go any farther after us and I swear upon my mother's grave, that at one point they even called out and seemed to beg us to

---

[†] The Colorado River as named by one of Coronado's captains, Hernando de Alarcon. It means the River of Good Guidance. McGinnies could not possibly have known that.

14

return to them. As if what they did offer was a better proposition than what did await us and now as I lie in the sands of this muddy valley I wonder if they were not right.

But eager to escape their harsh slavery we ignored their plea's and travelled on for many miles and soon ran out of water having but the one skin between us and it did not last long in the searing heat. We were roasted alive by the sun above and the shining ground beneath. There was some shade as we came into some rocky mountains and again found water. But it was bitter and salty. It might have been poison and yet we had to drink to have any chance of survival. The waters made us sick but we endured well enough to travel on. Besides a few cactus that we chopped into and ate pulp from we also found some small cactus growing in small bunches close to the ground. We were starving so we ate the bitter fruit‖ thereof. It too made us ill but travelled on because to stay put meant certain death.

There are no animals here, no sound, not a bird in the sky or the howl of a wolf in the night, the only other living things we saw were the flies. These were terrible giant things that buzzed at us and tried to suck our blood. I have never been afraid of any animal or insect but these were as big as hawks and I was sure that we should not survive their assault.

I will never forget how Francisco cried out as one drained him of blood. We only survived their frenzied attack because they flew away at dusk.

We moved on at night as swiftly as possible to get away from that evil place. Crossing a rocky ridge we found a valley with a muddy river flowing through it.

‖ Almost certainly Lophophora williamsii otherwise known as peyote.

Thanking St. Mary we rushed into the to drink our fill beneath the stars. The water not stagnant or nor bitter. Then Francisco gra shoulder and urged me from where we stood waist de the river, saying, "Espantosa!"

Eyes like yellow moons stared back at us from the surface. Hundreds of them. I scanned across the wide slow surface and saw that the water was black with their bodies, bodies that I could not tell what they were, though demonic undead things is all that comes to mind. We ran into the surrounding hills and felt blessed that no pursuit came of whatever those things were.

We were too weak to go any farther and one or the other of us kept a watch all night to see if the things approached but they did not.

When dawn rose we made our way cautiously to get more water as the heat of the day was dreadful. There was no sign of those creatures and we guessed for a time on what they could be. Alligators?

We lingered all day as the meadows nearby gave a sense of peace despite the terrifying evening. As dusk came on we kept our distance from the waters but heard strange cries thundering from upriver though we did not yet see what made the sounds. They echoed from the cliffs and we supposed that some unknown animal was calling to its mate.

Later well after midnight we heard them, the whispers. It was soft at first but gradually we all felt the malevolent whispers calling to us, telling us to go down to the waters and drink. We knew the power of El Diablo was in that place and most of us would not heed the whispers but Juan thought that perhaps an Indian child was near the water and he should save the child. We urged him not to go investigate but he did.

we lost sight of him in the
Dios!" from him, and a great
was no more. We never saw
hills again we did not sleep.

last our cactus buds and drank
of the river while one of us kept
there was no sign of the dark
the evil whispers but our strength
was ebbing not sure what to do. We are aliens
in this haunted land do not belong here anymore than
a fish does in the sky.

We determined that we could not remain in this place
despite the fresh water and trees. We went slowly up the
muddy stream until we came upon some ruins.

These were of very ancient make and we did determine
that whomever had made them were an evil race. Skulls
were scattered about the stone adobe walls like trophies and
there was an altar in the central square that looked like what
we had seen in Tenochtitlan for blood sacrifice. Still we did
investigate for some time, hoping to find some useful items
for ourselves.

We did find a crypt and did enter into it with some
trepidation. Inside were the bones of a warrior king and his
slaves. There were weapons of curious make, swords and
spears of an exceedingly hard bronze and we took them
despite their foul creators. There was a small amount of
treasure, a golden crown, a string of jewels for his necklace
and girdles of silver chain about his slave's bones, but we did
not take these for we were already so weak and considered
this place so cursed.

Gathering another supply of water to last us well into the
night, we ate some of the sweet grass from the meadow
hoping it would fill our aching bellies but I became sick from

it instead. We decided to spend the night in the ruin and go our way at daybreak.

On this night, we saw things move along the river banks, they glided along the edge of the shore, always just out of sight beside the mesquite trees so that we could not determine their shapes. But if there was a shape, I would say it was man-like.

These phantoms glided along the river bottom and creeped toward the ruin whenever the moons light was obscured by clouds. They gradually came closer and closer and their terrible whispers were driving us mad. We determined that they did seek our death. And if we remained this night they would surely have it.

We prayed to the Father and the Son, the Holy Ghost and the Virgin Mary to protect us, for we were indeed so weak I could not have fought them if I tried. Francisco pulled me to my feet and had us struggle to go farther into the hills and avoid the awful dark shapes.

Once out of the valley, the dark spirits remained behind and we were able to sleep among the tarantula, scorpion and snake.

Travelling on the next day, we kept the river on our right and moved northward because in the distance we thought it possible for better food. We knew every well how inhospitable it was behind us. By midday we saw shapes moving along the cliffs far the east and wondered if it might be some other Indians and thusly the chance for some food and provisions.

The shapes upon the cliffs saw us too.

We did learn what made those horrible cries of thunder.

Mighty winged birds cast of leather and bone did fly at us with cries that echoed across the canyon walls. They swooped down and we fought them as best we could with the swords and spears of brazen copper. But these monsters, these dragons were swift and clever, one would dive at us crying while another would silently swoop from behind and though we wounded several of them, they did take Don Hernandez away and rend him on the cliff face and allow their young to devour him utterly.

I shall forget his screams neither here nor in the afterlife.

We ran downriver to escape these thunderbirds of prey and took shelter in the ruins, which afforded some cover from their snapping beaks and rending claws.

I prayed then as I have never prayed before and did wonder at what I had done with my life to be so miserable and punished by the Lord God. My companions and I were but mere playthings for the demons of this world and each day one of us was taken away to our doom.

I did reflect upon my life and the many things I have done as recollected in the beginning of these last papers by my hand. And I can now look back at my life and admit that I have been a wicked man and am earning the torments of hell which is where I must surely be.

This is hell and I have been dead probably since I last saw Captain Alarcon and I was captured by the red-skinned natives. For life could not be this maddening on its own.

It is my hope that I may atone and be done with this purgatory and move to the next circle but I have no way of knowing the day nor the hour of my punishments. It is but a vicious cycle of day and night but with endless sweltering heat and cruel judgments inflicted by various skulking demons and flying devils.

We last two remain in the ruins haunted though they may be and as night falls I know that the whisperers in the dark will again tempt us with death.

I fell asleep.

WHISPERS OUT OF THE DUST — DAVID J. WEST

When I awoke my last countryman and companion Francisco de la Vaca had vanished. I searched the ruins over and found no trace of him. I hunted along the river and there was nothing to indicate where he could have gone, no tracks, no sign, no hint of his departure. His clothing was gone but anything he had carried remained near his bedroll. I must confess that I wonder if he did not decide to end the madness by going and accepting the death that the whisperers did offer. But surely he could have told me that he was done? I could have ended his mortal journey with my lance or saber? Why not tell me? I felt blessed at the least that the terrible thunderbirds did not return but what if they had snatched him up in the night? What if they horrible dark spirits in the river did drown him? I may never know. And that horror of not knowing may be the worst of all.

I hunted for something to eat beyond the simple sweet grasses and sage that pollute this hell. I found grubs and they were truly a feast of hell, writhing in my mouth, I found some few hard seeds in a basket within the ruin but found that I could not chew them unless they were boiled and then there were palatable.

I was finding in could survive in this hell. But did I really want to? I did not wish to remain here but felt trapped by the desert to the south and the thunderbirds to the north. What other way could I go?

As I was preparing for the night and fortifying my camp in the ruins, I heard a sound of someone walking, dragging their feet in an awkward shuffle. I looked through the outcropping of stone and did see my friend Francisco! He appeared lost, confused in the darkness, I called to him in joy never had I been so happy to see another person.

He jerked awkwardly and moved closer to me and then as the moonlight splashed across his face I saw that he was a ruin of man. Covered in worms, scabs and sores he should not have been alive and yet when I saw his eyes I saw that there was no life in them.

Struggling over stones among the ruins his broken jaws champed for my blood and I ran him through with the saber and yet, he did not die!

I fled through the ruins and he came after me in a slow steady manner, I hit him with a great block that I could hardly lift and his chest was broken, and yet he stood back up and again came on.

There was nothing I could do, this was madness, this was death and I would not face it. I ran to the hills under the moon to be away. I ran until my legs gave out and I collapsed in dust and I knew no more.

I awoke at daybreak and came to my senses just as Francisco was almost upon me. He was undead and yet moved on hungering for my blood. As I have said before this was the worst of hells I could imagine. There is no rest in hell, no relief just the unending chase and torment.

I had lost my weapons gained from the tomb of the ancients and was again with naught but my hands to face this demon of hell. I was growing weaker from lack of food and knew that I could not continue one much farther like this. I resolved that this wretched existence had to end, but I could not allow myself to become as Francisco and damned for all time.

He was relentless but none too fast. I decided I would trap him and let the madness end. I found that if I ran up to the ruins he would follow and I could sneak away to the far end of the valley and have enough time to sleep a couple hours and then be ready for him again. In moving like this I spent a couple of awful days and nights. At each end of the valley I made a stack of stones in preparation for tumbling over the top of him and trapping him. I suppose I could feel blessed that so long as he pursued me I did not see the thunderbirds or the dark shapes in the water that had so tormented me. Perhaps the devil was being cruel to be kind? I have no answers.

The final time I slept, I awoke to Francisco gripping and biting my leg. I screamed and kicked but his rotten hands were strong as steel and his teeth burned as the forge.

I managed to escape him but was weak and wounded. I am sure that I was poisoned. I dragged myself away and was able to only just keep ahead of my hungry pursuer.

I have set myself against the towering pile of stone that I meant to knock down upon him and I write these last few lines. My leg wound burns and is turning black and it has only been I think a few hours. This is indeed the end of this hell and soon I will drop this cairn down upon us both. Perhaps I can atone for my life here in the next one.

Vaya con Dios for I cannot:
Sincerely Diego de la Vega Matamoros.

Final statement on the matter by Elias McGinnies

I shared this record I have found with the others here and we did all marvel and wonder at the horror of it.

We did go and examine the ruins of which Matamoros spoke but we could find no tomb or crypt. There was a wide assortment of pottery and the like some rotten skins and bones equaling habitation but not since ancient times I suppose. Where these people went I do not care to know for the whole of the ruins did have an air of evil and foreboding about it and I care not one whit to return to it.

We did also cautiously approach the cliffs he mentioned housing thunderbirds but found nothing there either save for a wide protuberance of bones equaling as if there had been quite a slew of predators in the area at one time but thankfully no longer.

I am certainly not saying Matamoros was a liar as his bones are a true and final testament to his tale but perhaps some things were not as he supposed and the deseret can drive men to madness. Still I did do some things just in case.

We put the cursed bones I collected from the cairn, presumably both Matamoros and Francisco, and rather than worry any more about what might come of them, I did put them all on a raft that I had the Bishop bless and we did send them down the Virgin River which soon feeds the Colorado and from then on to the sea. May that far place bring them peace and have their ghosts leave my fields alone.

"It always is Christmas Eve, in a ghost story."
— Jerome K. Jerome

Stranger Come Knocking

Anonymous[†], December 25th, 1865

"It was the coldest of remembered evenings and we were gathered about the fire, singing carols of pleasantries, Christmas and such when a stranger come knocking upon our door but said he nothing more.

I went and answered, saying 'I trust you have need of something friend, enter eat, drink and be of good cheer'.

But of a man or woman or child there was none near.

Shutting the door, I was given pause and more, on who could have been knocking there at our door. The children were hushed and all drew near as yet another knock came and this time to the rear.

Thinking they had passed by too quickly from the front to the back, I called out, 'You're welcome here Jack come and join us and celebrate the New Year and Christmas time snack'.

But when I rose to the door, there again was no one more. Alone was the threshold and cold still moon waiting for someone to show their face soon.

[†] While this poem is uncredited, it was likely based upon a rumored incident that happened to the Thomas Carlyle family in that same year.

Back to our song and verse and feast, when all of a sudden the knocking increased.

The call at first to join was unheeded, but the curiosity was yet unneeded for we felt a chill and a crawling as boot steps walked cross the floor, though no one was seen entering our rear door.

The tramp was weighty and the presence felt, by all in the home who therein truly dwelt.

T'was asked, who goes there, here in my house, your steps do frighten my children and spouse.

Silence met us, for none answered my speech and then when we smelt his brimstone odor, then did we screech as it as it spoke meeting our ear, saying and I quoth, "I am here."

Under the tree and through the cupboards did the children run and hide, with this now unwelcome guest I did in vain attempt to collide.

But of his material there was none, I crashed through him and t'was no fun, to be cast off like a shoe and have the dinner table given me stars for a view.

The plates were smashed and Christmas hopes dashed as the dogs did bark and the flames went out—all to the last spark. We were trapped in the gloom and crushing dark while he laughed at us as if on a lark.

The lights of Christmas were dimmed and gone as our hopes too were smashed and suddenly withdrawn. And I never thought that I was a coward until that hour when I was trapped there within the Devils power.

And then as all faith was lost and to the point of exhaust, did my little baby girl open her mouth and let loose all we had taught her in a whirl.

She said her prayer loud and true that we might come safely through, and to the devil she said to leave and go, that we might never have to know him again, as above and so below.

The Devil did heed the spawn of my seed, as she called on the angels of Heaven and Jesus to save us from he who had so cruelly seized us.

Like a hurricane he did depart, and never did it swell so strong my heart, for that brave little girl with her gospel art. She showed us the way, brave and true and to utterly convey just what to do.

So if a stranger come knocking (and he will) careful who you invite without first talking, know their light, or you could be in for quite a terrible late Christmas fright."

"Was this Hades, Sheole, or the place for the condign punishment of the wicked, or was it the grand sewer for the waste and filth of vast animation?"
— Illegible name 1865

Curse of the Lost City

Asa Christiansen's Journal
— **May 3rd 1866**

We have arrived at the place of our calling within the Muddy Mission[. St. Thomas; a grand home of opportunity, a veritable land for newcomers as the prophet so eloquently spoke, what seems only a fortnight ago.

Mary Ann thinks it a queer name for a settlement of Saints[. Brother Brizby said it was named for Brother Thomas S. Smith who managed to save the necks of the initial lucky thirteen pioneers on more than one occasion and more than earned being called Saint Thomas and having the town named for him. He is now also the Bishop.

I reminded Mary Ann of St. George, named for Apostle George A. Smith, yet she still thinks it a queer name.

We selected a site for our home on the southwest edge. I set up our tent and will begin work on a cistern and fence on the morrow. With any luck and blessings in heaven we shall start our garden and a crop of cotton soon. With this

---

[Mormon designation for the territory.
[A Mormon term for themselves, making everyone else within the church also Brother or Sister. Being a Saint does not necessarily mean everyone else is a sinner, but it helps.

hot weather and abundant water I hope to have a better season than any possible up north in Salt Lake. I told father I would grow the biggest watermelons he had ever seen, when he comes this fall.

— May 4th

I had to ask for some meager supplies from Bishop Smith as we lost more than I thought in the many Virgin River crossings. Also lost my mule and had to spend day looking for him. I could not find him and fear he was stolen and eaten by the Paiutes or has expired in the desert.

— May 5th

I retrieved my mule. It had run north along the hills until it came to a large meadow of sweet grass near some ruins. I explored them for a time looking to find any artifacts or useful items from the ancient inhabitants of this land.

Brother Brizby informed me afterward that the place has been dubbed 'The Lost City' by the Saints. He also cautioned that I ought to stay away from it as even the Paiutes would not go near. They said their ancient enemies had built it long ago and were now gone and to good riddance. But there was no reason to worry over it now.

I found it to be quite the curious setting, some few walls stood out against the sun, granting some of the only shade to be had in the entire valley, and several more were toppled over. All was of adobe make with some small amount of lumber for bracing and interior strength not unlike what the Saints are doing in St. Thomas as lumber here is scarce. I found quite a few potsherds and some large bones of an animal that I cannot discern. There were some weathered stones with a swirling venomous writing upon them that I could not understand. I moved one of the larger of these stones as it seemed to be a lid of some kind, but as I lifted it, a scorpion crawled upon my hand and I dropped the stone lid.

I brushed the scorpion off and received no sting, but the stone broke as it landed, lending not a fragment to be recovered or to be shown to another soul so that we might someday understand its meaning.

Beneath the now broken lid was indeed a stone sarcophagus or box. I carefully removed the fragments watching for more scorpions or snakes and found not but a few interesting artifacts that I took home. It was now getting dark and as I had no lantern I returned home. I will explore the ruin more when I have time after getting to my responsibilities.

— May 7th

Strange dreams plague my mind. I hear whispers in the dark, whispers from the dust of this forgotten land, they do call to me and tell me to take my place among them.

— May 8th

I took Brother Brizby with me to the ruins today and asked if he could hear what I have heard.

Alas, he could not. He must not be a true Saint.

He reminded me of what Old Bishop and the others have said of the place and even likened it to old cursed Chorazin of the Bible. But if he cannot hear the spirit when it calls what does he really know of anything?

I tried to show him what I had discovered, all that I had learned but he would not join me. I say let them who have eyes see and them with ears hear and lo, all in this city of St. Thomas seem to be deaf and dumb to what is beneath their very feet!

I have no more time for this journal or the records of mere men. There is so much more out there waiting to be fulfilled!

Mary Ann Christiansen's Journal
— May 6th

I hear Asa's whistle! He is coming home! Asa remembered his prayers and found our runaway mule. I am so grateful to the Lord that the Indians did not eat him. Asa also brought home a few relics from some ancient place. One has an evil countenance about it, resembling nothing so much as a demonic frog. Asa laughed when I told him but he said it was but an old Indian idol of perhaps make from the days of the Nephites and Lamanites.

It gave me an uncomfortable feeling and whether or not Mother will come remains to be seen, but I shan't wish her to look upon such a grotesque abomination.

It is my hope that in time we can raise a family here despite the trials and tribulations of this haunted and barren land. Asa's relic is watching me as I write these words. How I fear its cross and carven eyes. They stare like a goats with black crosses upon a yellow field. I asked Asa again to remove it from our home, soon, he said before putting it back in a burlap sack.

The dog [Rufus] will not come inside despite Asa's best whistle.

— May 7th

Have proceeded with mending of the sisters clothing that was ruined in the fire outside the Low's foundation today. Still waiting on Asa to start work on our home, he has been unwell and spent his time either in our tent or at the ruins. He still has the toad by his bedside. I do hope he gets rid of the thing as he promised. Our faithful dog [Rufus] which used to adore Asa will not come near him now.

— May 8th

Asa still has not started work on our cistern or garden as he has spent almost all his days here on the Muddy Mission at the Lost City ruins. I had Brother Brizby go with him to try and talk to him about our family's needs, I have had to walk to Brother and Sister Bonelli's for water. Asa is a good man but far too curious for his or our own good. I pray he comes to his senses soon. Our dog [Rufus] has run away, I fear the Indians will eat him if he does not succumb to the heat and perish.

— May 9th

I have tried to get Asa to abandon his obsession with The Lost City ruins but he will not listen to me. I shall ask the brethren to intervene on my behalf.

— May 10th

Asa sleeps outside now as I have told him I will not have his poor behavior in my home. It is just a tent but it is still mine. I am heartbroken at his indifference. He seems to care more for his findings at the ruins than he does for me, his wife! If the situation is not changed and soon, I will leave this godforsaken place and return to my father. I have again asked the brethren to speak with Asa.

— May 11th

Wonderful Brother Brizby has helped begin our cistern without Asa's help. He hired a few Paiutes to help dig and they soon reached water having only gone down the height of a man. Mayhaps Asa will be shamed into returning to our family!

— May 12th

I went to fetch water this morning and Horror! The cistern was full of toads! This has not been a problem at anyone else's homestead and I was mortified. Brother Brizby fetched a pair of Paiutes who had dug the cistern and said that perhaps they would collect the animals and consider it a good sign, as they would eat the creatures. However once they arrived, the Paiutes would not touch the foul creatures declaring them to be some sign of calamity and they spoke of the Anasazi, their Ancient Enemy.

When Asa returned home, he laughed and showed me his toad idol once again and he commanded the toads to leave the cistern and they did! It was as if he was Pied Piper of Hamlet[10]. Asa led them toward the ruins of the Lost City at twilight and they followed him like a mad legion. I however would not follow him.

— May 13th

Wonderful news! Our faithful dog Rufus has returned. I can barely restrain myself from his kisses as I write this I am reminded of happier days. I hear Asa's whistle, he has returned . . .

Daniel Rutledge's Journal

— May 11th

As I had told Sister Christiansen I would, I spoke today with Brother Asa Christiansen up at The Lost City ruins. He was not interested in my reminding him of his familial responsibilities or otherwise. He asked me several times if I could hear anything and I replied each time with 'only the wind' and he laughed a rather humorless chuckle at that each time and finally said something about knowing where he stood with me and the brethren.

Thank the Lord, he has not fallen away from the gospel however, proclaiming that he has a greater knowledge of the truth of it than any man within The Muddy Mission. He spoke for a time on the Nephites, Lamanites and more so

---

[10] She must have meant Hamelin.

on the Gadianton Robbers[11] that used to inhabit this land. He is far more of a scriptorian than I would have ever imagined. I could have sworn that Sister Christiansen said he had not gone to schooling but he knew more than I had ever heard before in regards to the history of this land. He spoke of where perhaps the Robbers had held their ancient rites and vigils of sacrifice and depravity, and where they would imbue idols of stone with awful powers to use as conduits to the profane and diabolic.

I cautioned him to not delve too deeply into those subjects but he laughed once again saying it was but to better study the ways and means of the enemy. I also reminded him to not neglect his family and keep his shoulder to the wheel. He laughed, but told me he understood very well and that I should not fret for his soul, that it was well claimed.

— May 13th

Brother Asa Christiansen was attacked by his missing dog this evening when he returned home from The Lost City ruins. We shot the dog but he was viciously mauled. We were not sure if the dog had gone mad or not, as it had been friendly with Sister Christiansen just prior to Brother Christiansen's arrival.

Brother Christiansen has a severe fever and we expect the worst. It is too perilous to try and remove him back to St. George to see Dr. Adams[12] with so many Virgin River crossings. We blessed him and all present in the circle felt as if his spirit passed from him though he still lived. We prepare for what would be our second funeral in St. Thomas.

---

[11] All three, Nephites, Lamanites and Gadianton Robbers are peoples mentioned in the Book of Mormon.
[12] Doc Adams later known for the Lost Adams Diggings gold mine.

— May 16th

I have decided that despite Sister Christiansen's statements, malaria must have played a major part in Brother Christiansen's behavior of late but it is indeed a curious thing.

In the evening, Brother Christiansen awoke after three days of sleep. He is healing well and in much better spirits than the last time I spoke with him. He sleeps often still and is troubled in the night according to Sister Christiansen but will recover fine I think. He spoke somewhat of the Lost City ruins and how he will never go back as he is sure they are the cursed remains of a Gadianton outpost.

He then reached into a bag beside his bedroll and did then throw a small stone idol of a toad out of his tent when he recovered himself. Sister Christiansen declared that it was not nearly far enough away. She did beg me to throw it in the river for them and be rid of it forever. I went to fetch it, to do as she had asked but I could not find it in the darkness, though it should have been right outside their tent flap. Perhaps it must have bounced into their cistern though the lid was fast upon it. I did see a live toad hopping away but it was assuredly not the same one that he threw for everyone that had seen it knew it to be but a statue or idol of some kind. To ease her mind, I told her that I had found it and would dispose of it.

— May 17th

I looked for the toad idol again when first daylight came but there was no sure sign of it. I have decided that there is nothing to it, but I shall ask all of our folk to stay away from and forget the ruins anyhow. I'll send a team of men to knock down the walls and we will bury the foundations thereof and never speak of them again. If people don't talk

...all just go away and be forgotten as it should

...ost City ruins are buried and gone. We will speak no more of them.

— May 20th

I went back to the ruins today, and could swear I heard a whisper on the wind calling to me.

I shall come again tomorrow.

"Take my word for it, there is no such thing as an ancient village, especially if it has seen better days, unillustrated by its lengths of terror."
— J. S. LeFanu

Skullduggery

Letter from Angus Call to his sister: August 30th, 1866

My Dearest Elizabeth

Ever since Brother Rutledge's abrupt disappearance two months ago under mysterious but likely enough circumstances, folk have been nervous about goings on here. Some say it was the Indians but others think different. Some say an evil spirit haunts this valley and we should take care when out and about. I've heard it said that if our eyes could but see them, the world is as thick with spirits as the sands of the sea and that we are never truly alone.

But I try to keep a rational approach and not worry over every little thing though most all of the people here are a superstitious lot by nature especially the Indians themselves. I do think myself level headed and worthy of being an reasonable minded individual and that is why I am so precisely vexed by what I will soon relate and I do humbly indulge your patience and ask for you to take my word at what I relate and say herein. That I am not prone to flights of fancy and such has made all of this that much more horrifying.

As you know from previous correspondence we have a salt mine some five miles south of us. It does take some work to get the salt but it is most useful to have such access in any case. There has alas been some accidents though, we blasted a portion of a ledge free to get the salt and while gathering the free clumps, we had a collapse I barely escaped with my life and almost right beside me, a poor Mr. Redway was buried. We dug him out as fast as possible but he was certainly dead and horribly mangled.

The Paiutes took this to be a particularly bad sign, as if his death wasn't a bad enough thing in and of itself, and in the terrible commotion and rockslide along with the extracting of Mr. Redway, he lost his head under a particularly large boulder that we were unable to yet move and therefore retrieve his crushed skull. It was truly a gruesome sight and I only tell you because it pertains to the incident in question that I will come to in good time. So please forgive the thought of gore and bloody mishap.

To further the trouble with the superstitious Paiutes, the very next day what comes walking into St. Thomas but a camel!

The Paiute's panicked and fled for the most part believing it to be a manifestation of the great spirit come to punish them for wickedness (their thievery no doubt).

It took some time to coax them into coming back to St. Thomas and renewing their much needed labors in the fields. I was to find out from Brother Leithead later that the rogue camel must have come from a dromedary line operating between Lost Angeles and Fort Mojave. Apparently some of the salt freighters had the bright idea to use the desert animals, I can't say I blame the thought process but the camels feet were torn asunder by the rough American stone, and this is all besides horses becoming almost as frightened of camels beside them as the Paiute. So Brother Leithead told me that the camels were let loose to fend for themselves. How queer. I should much like to capture one and see if I couldn't use it for myself. Can you see your dear brother now? Riding along like a Raj of the desert?

But I have drifted off course dear sister.

Not long after Mr. Redway's death, I found a need to head back to the salt mine at dusk and gain another portion of salt for myself, as I would be able to sell it for a very good price to a Mr. Fenton who claimed he needed it post haste and was busy with other Indian Bureau matters in Rioville. Not wishing to work in the hot sun nor take away from my many other responsibilities at home I took the wagon and went to the mine.

It was getting dark but there was enough light from both my lantern and the moon that I didn't worry about seeing to my task. So, I went about my task and what should happen but here of all places, we had clouds roll in and obscure the moon light, then I was left but to my lamp to see by and the queerest thing began to happen, I started to hear footsteps round about me but no one spoke and there was never anyone that I could see.

I continued my work of shoveling out the salt from the earth and my lanterns flame did flicker and waver, as if something was trying to snuff it out. I can't tell you how worried I became at this but as it did not go out entirely I persevered and kept at my work. I did also continue to hear footsteps but again no one was anywhere to be found and I kept at my task.

A cool wind had come up during this time and yet my lamp should have been wind proof and yet it sputtered as if fighting against fingers pinching at the wick.

As I was digging out the salt, I felt a tap at my shoulder, but I knew no one was there so I ignored the sensation and set about my task all the harder, though now I will admit to you that I was vexed and worried at these happenings. I tell you this as I was so sure it was but my imagination, there was no possibility of anyone being at my shoulder in that inhospitable place at that time of night. No, I knew it had to be my imagination.

Then what had once been a tap became a full poke!

I was surely frightened at the suddenness at the late hour, the eerie stillness and now the rude interruption. I wheeled about to face my antagonist and who was there but a ghastly headless apparition holding a bucket outstretched to me!

It did beckon to me to examine the bucket of which I fearfully did and inside looking up at me was Mr. Redway's gruesome head!

His body stood there as though standing and waiting for something, I know not what. I tried to back away but he followed me, gesturing as if for me to take the bucket but such a thing I would not do for I was afraid that I might catch my death as one might catch a cold.

And Elizabeth please believe my incredible frightening story, he had the most ghastly look upon his face, as though choked with dirt and soil and oh, so much pain. He stood there holding the bucket with such an accusing face within and I begged my pardon in a hoarse whisper and bid him leave me be.

I backed away and he followed me and the horror of escaping that headless body and bucket with such a terrible face. Oh, and those eyes, an awful cold paleness that gave no hint of depth or love, they were rolled back up into his ghostly skull and his tongue it wagged out like a worm escaping the grave. I was near to faint and I ran to the wagon and still he followed after me, all the while waggling the bucket at me like a man might offer you a drink.

WHISPERS OUT OF THE DUST — DAVID J. WEST

I whipped the horses and still that grim specter followed me. I screamed at him to leave me be that I had naught to do with his demise but still he pursued me, beckoning that I should take that dreadful bucket with his head.

But no I would do no such thing at all!

Whipping the horses to a furious pace I screamed and wailed to leave me be but every time I looked back he was still there shaking his bucket, as if pleading that I should take hold of that awful pail!

Carried home by good horses, my wife said I was quivering in a heap upon the buckboards floor and that there was no sign of Mr. Redway at all. And she said that there was no sign of anyone at all and she did keep a good watch throughout the night saying that I was indeed in a state of hysterics and in such poor health that she did think to call for the doctor but I cried that I wanted nothing so much as to get some good sleep and be well by morning.

So I explain all of this to you in the event that you hear of my strange cowardice and panic, for I know that folk are wont to talk such things about the late night Sunday joint. Rest assured that I have not lost my mind and that I am guiltless when it comes to that poor man's death and dismemberment.

But in the light of day I did begin to feel for the poor deceased gentile[13] Mr. Redway and I took some Paiutes who had been given quite a bit of liquid courage[14] and did set to work moving the massive boulder that had hidden away Mr. Redway's head.

---

[13] Mormon designation for a non-member.
[14] Undoubtedly this would have been Valley Tan whiskey. A favorite beverage made in Salt Lake Valley.

We had to spend the better part of the day at the task and were finally able to extract that wretched crushed collection of bone and scalp.

I did join these items with the already buried body of Mr. Redway in the town cemetery and no more such sighting and hauntings have been reported since.

I did sincerely feel for the man and felt ashamed that I had to be so very spooked to see to it that he was fully and completely laid to rest. I have certainly learned my lesson and shan't shirk these matters ever again.

Your brother

Angus Call

"It shows me, that the adversary is trying to prevent me from going; but I am going all the same if I have to walk every foot of the way."
— *Samuel Claridge[15] 1864*

The Big Mouth

Statement of William Webb: June 12th, 1867

A company of men and I were digging a well on the outskirts of town. It was blazing hot and I recall that I joked and laughed that if we didn't find water soon we wouldn't be climbing out of that hole. Somebody reminded me that I had claimed I could dig the well faster than anyone of them. This wasn't the first time I had been accused of having a big mouth.

We did however strike water at twelve feet and proceeded to line the well. As we were taking a short break for lunch a thirsty horse wandered into camp.

Taking a few moments we wondered at whose it was and we both fed and watered it as it looked pretty rough from coming in off the desert. I tied it up thinking that it must have been lost from someone in town and would soon enough appreciate that we had found it. After an hour and with the well nearly complete the others joked that I should go looking for its owner since I surely had the biggest mouth and could call out the loudest to find the owner. I laughed, I can take a joke. I took it out and went looking on my own mule for the owner. No one was missing a horse and that

---

[15] Samuel Claridge was one of the first settlers of St. Thomas.

made me wonder at what may have happened so I took off down the high desert road with a large cask of water and my biggest skin.

About a half mile from town I came upon the ruined body of a boy lying dead from the blistering heat of the sun. Beside him was an empty canteen and a parched dry keg. He was bloated and a ruinous mess. There was no way I could tell who he was.

I buried him beside the road and did put up a headboard denoting him as best I could so that others might know who he was at a later date.

Guessing that there was more to this than a lone boy I went on further down the track toward St. George. Passing along a horrid waterless stretch of desert I soon came upon the Davison's, husband and wife. I called to them as he could see them leaning together sitting beneath a sheet that they had stretched out to protect them from the sun. I could also see that their wagon had lost a wheel and was broke down beside the road.

I regretted having to inform them of what must surely have been an untimely end to their son when I realized they were not answering my hallo.

They were dead as well, parched and dried from the awful sun. They only son must have tried to get back to town for water but passed away.

Then I noticed something, they still had kegs of water. Two big barrels were strapped to the sides of their wagon and yet here they lie dry and dead as bones when the water for life was right beside them.

Why didn't they drink? Why didn't they use what they had?

That thought plagued me night and day pretty near every time I thought on water for the next few weeks. Their salvation was right at hand and yet they ignored it and died. I wonder what could have done such a thing to their minds and I am determined to never let it happen again.

Everybody else says that sometimes bad things happen to good people that it is just the Lords will or perhaps it was their time to go but I hate that.

Some peoples answers said that it was the evil spirits that haunt this land a causing them to believe their kegs had run dry and still others have said that perhaps their water had gone bad and they daren't drink but that was untrue on account of I drank some of that water myself and didn't feel a thing sideways.

Wasn't too long until everyone told me I needed to keep my big mouth shut about the affair and let people going on living their lives. We can't fix all tragedies and alleviate the world of its mysteries. The Bishop even cautioned me about delving too deep into the mysteries but I don't cotton to that attitude even if I do have a big mouth. No, there had to be something sinister about it all and I aim to find out.

Ever time I wanted to know something I set out to knows it. So I prepared a way just as the good Lord prepared a way for me to find out.

I took the old Indian we call Old Bishop[16] with me and we rode out that way one evening under a leaden sky and camped just to try and understand a spell.

Now Old Bishop he is a wise old man and we call him Old Bishop on account of him looking kinda like Bishop Shaffer down in Provo. He has always been a good hand too watching over our cattle at night on the long trek southwards.

---

[16] There was a Ute near Provo who was also referred to as "Old Bishop" because of his resemblance to a local bishop.

Now Old Bishop he did some preparing before we went out. He burnt some sacred smoke, sage and I don't know what else and had us waft it around our bodies and be cleansed he called it and then when we got out on the parched road close to where the Davison's had passed we made camp. Old Bishop he made a great circle around our camp and he kept up his singing and drumming for some time. I don't reckon most of my fellow saints would have cottoned to this type of service but then I like to see what else the world has to offer too.

The stars came out in the great vault above us casting a mysterious glow across the pale desert. There weren't much wind and not a bird or coyote did we hear, deathly silence all about and that's when Old Bishop told me that we wasn't alone.

He kept up on his song and drum and I sat there casting twigs into a tiny fire that I kept just for a small amount of light. I have to tell you that as I sat inside the circle, I didn't feel nothing, nothing bad and nothing good neither I was just enjoying myself and thinking that while this was good to spend time with Old Bishop this was a fool's errand and ain't nothing gonna come of it.

Well, sirree was I wrong.

I had to get up to shake the dew of the lilies or talk to man about a horse however you like to put it and I stood up and not wanting to do anything right next to where I eat so to speak I stepped outside of Old Bishop's circle.

I took a good few steps beyond and looked into the dark beyond. Stars were out there but their light was so far away, so cold.

I finished my business and turned around to walk on back into camp when something seized my heart.

A coldness I have never known touched right inside my

soul like great claws were a squeezing it and telling me to give up, to lay right down and die.

I could hear my heartbeat thumping in my chest or was it Old Bishop's drum? I don't know.

I strained to take a step and that's when I turned just a mite and saw what had seized my heart.

A great ghostly thing, a looking like an Indian chief with a big old war bonnet—but his mouth, Lord, his mouth was about five times too big with teeth like sabers just a grinning at me like he was about to eat my heart! His cold claw like fingers were twisting at my breast and he whispered to me to lay down and die, but I weren't about to give up jus yet.

I tried to call out to Old Bishop for some help, I tried with everything I could to cry but no words came and the squeezing just grew a stronger and harder and that horrible ghost mouth just laughed like silent thunder.

He loomed over me and opened all the wider like he was gonna devour me whole. He had me wrapped up like a rat with a bull snake and I should'a been just as much a goner. But I remembered the words my old pap had always told me true.

Then I prayed as I had never prayed before to be saved from this hell and this devils power. I spoke the words I had always been taught but never used before and Lo! It worked and I stepped out of that grim demons grasp back into the circle.

Old Bishop was watching the whole time. He now stopped his song and drumming and took a drink of water. I was breathing hard and heavy and felt surprisingly cold for such a hot summer evening. I tried to tell Old Bishop what I had just experienced but he just nodded and looked on as usual.

Maybe you don't understand, I said, I was just attacked

by that ghost mouth thing.

Old Bishop he turned and looked at me and smiled, then he said, "You wanted to know what was out here. You wanted to see it and thus you invited it. But you had the power to deny the Ghost Mouth and I knew you could. It is well. We have shown him that he cannot do any more harm to us and he must leave us alone, but this is his trail and we should not use it anymore and let the others know to avoid it too and go upon the low road.

And that was all he would say about it. We never talked about it again but I know that he could see what I saw and that that big ghost mouth is still out there waiting to snatch anyone who uses his trail.

"The snake is monarch here. Let him live to enjoy his majesty undisturbed by us..., and since I have got out of there I do not expect to ever intrude upon his imperial majesty's dominions again."

— George W. Brimhall: 1865

<u>Gods of the Old Land</u>

Last record written by Seneca Howland[17]: August 30th, 1869

To Whom it May Concern[18]:

I, Seneca Howland, write these lines with the realization that I will soon die, but I wish that perhaps some word of what happened to us may yet reach some civilized ears and that we may someday have prayers over our graves rather than be left to wander as ghosts in this Christian god forsaken land. I say Christian god forsaken because he holds no dominion here compared to the old ones who still dwell in this place. This truly is a haunted land you who come after me, best take care of what you disturb herein.

---

[17] Seneca Howland was a member of Major John Wesley Powell's exploration of the Colorado River and Grand Canyon area in the summer of 1869.

[18] While the events this rare and precious document explains are not within the Moapa valley proper [the essential story of this book] it is directly related as per being one of the documents I found in the collection and only came to light because of the fortuitous actions of a St. Thomas resident.

WHISPERS OUT OF THE DUST — DAVID J. WEST

I did strive with my brother Oramel[19], and Mr. Dunn to remain with Major Powell and see whether we would not make it out of the canyon and to the civilization that would meet us downriver. My brother rather said that No, we should go overland to St. George, as only death awaited us on that treacherous river. He was sure that the rapids would only get worse and we should lose all of our lives. He did tell Major Powell that is was madness to continue but when an agreement could not be reached he declared we should part ways. We were near starving, these supplies having been ruined by the waters and soon enough we would become stranded and starve if we remained. I did not like this and wished to remain with Major Powell but felt I had to stand with my brother.

We refused the rotten rations offered us, took our skins full of water and proceeded to try and climb up and out of the canyon.

It was hard going as the canyon walls were very tall and jagged and the heat was truly oppressive. We had reached quite a height and did see Major Powell and the others as they drifted out of sight down the rough river.

It was night on dusk and we were yet only about midway up the canyon. As we searched for an ideal ledge or spot to camp for the night we found some flagstones that were wholly unexpected. They did seem more like carven stairs rather than what at first we believed were simply broken stone and we followed the curious path around a small fissure that opened to reveal a square cut cavern. There was a wide large shelf just below that I did imagine kept this

---

[19] O. G. Howland had been tasked with mapping the river and taking notes.

opening hidden from view of the river and nearly all directions. This was truly a secret entrance.

Now there was no denying that this was indeed manmade and carved by some skilled ancient hand. But who they were and to what end we could not yet say. We decided we should investigate this most serendipitous find and see what value may come of it. And yes, perhaps even treasure we hoped.

We lit our single lantern and ventured inside. The tunnel was such that we could easily walk abreast of each other and the ceiling overhead was higher than we could reach. We followed the passage for some hundred yards until chambers opened up on either side. These were big rooms with water containers, now with but dust in the bottom. There were several torches we could ignite to light our way so as to expend all of our own fuel. Further on we came to a crossroads of sorts with a great idol at its center. It had a coy and mystic look upon its Asian or Egyptian type face and scandalous golden body of exaggerated feminine proportions. It was seated and there were some few smaller relics cast about it, idols and strange copper tools. We had never seen such a thing before and were in awe of its most curious existence.

It is times like this that you may realize that what you thought you knew of the world is indeed a very small thing in relation to the whole article.

We took a passage to the left and ended up in a chamber that looked to have been a barracks or perhaps a kitchen at one time. In a central area a small stream of water was channeled through a carven spout, it was not unpleasant to the taste. There was also a shelf space with all the implements one might need in a mess hall. The utensils however were very large and seemed as if they were meant for hands much larger than our own. Bowls and plates that would appear more like platters to us were strewn about the room and soon we did also find several large granaries full of dry seeds and beans.

Though many did not look familiar to us, we thought we might take a chance at cooking them and did proceed to begin boiling some water upon a furnace area with a ventilation shaft leading up and away. Some large ones were quite tasty once they were thoroughly boiled but we could not crack them open until cooking[20].

Once we had eaten and felt somewhat refreshed we continued our exploration of the caverns. Past the crossroads with the idol we found a shrine to gigantic old gods or mummies. These were adorned with gold and armor and it was here that we noticed that the walls were also covered with hieroglyphic writing that we in no way could interpret. This was surely the find of the century. A civilization that had once inhabited these desolate places and with a writing system that might tell of whom they were and what became of them.

I mentioned that we might ought to make some scratching or perhaps rubbings of some of these characters but Oramel said we hadn't enough paper left to us to record these things but that we should perhaps mark the outside entrance in such a way that we alone could find it again from the top of the mesa and that for now we should just take what wealth we could. I had not mentioned that I still had these few sheets in my own possession as of yet.

The huge gods in this shrine were taller yet than any of us by a span. The golden breastplates upon their chests were carven with strange creatures and dragons and I did wonder

---

[20] These are almost certainly palm seeds of the Washingtonia filifera.

at how long an age they had lain here. There was a stone box nearby and when we pried it open, expecting treasure we were disappointed to find it held only sheets of lead with more curious writings upon it. There were also some strange deteriorating skins and bones but what creature they could have come from we had no idea. Something exceedingly large.

Close by there also appeared to be a dais or bench of some sort. It was more than big enough for several people to sit beside each other or perhaps for a man to lay down upon, albeit uncomfortably and in such a manner as one would be arching their stomach and breast forward more than the head and feet. Grooves along the side became channels that culminated in a collection point at the top and we realized in horror that it was indeed a sacrificial altar for the collection of blood for the appeasement to some eldritch god of death.

I already had an uncomfortable feeling being in this wicked place but the others insisted we ought to look for some possible treasures and such especially since we were now in no short supply of food or water.

We decided to explore the opposite tunnel that led deeper into the mountain. Here there were no more torches along the wall and the dark seemed especially oppressive and the air too was heavy and smelt of reptiles. I wondered if it was full of a fetid gas but Mr. Dunn and Oramel were both very intent on finding some treasure that they were sure must exist on account of these ancient undiscovered peoples.

Moving deeper within I thought our lantern might be snuffed out by the amorphous darkness. Mr. Dunn said he would go back and get another torch, saying he had confidence he could make it back on his own in the dark since it was indeed such a wide easy passage and only some few hundred yards back to both the shrine and mess hall chambers. Against my better judgment we split up, Oramel and myself going forward.

The lantern seemed to only illuminate weakly here and I could but see only a foot or so in front of each step while Oramel walked slowly beside me. We saw more glyphs upon the walls and here and there passed more bones and tattered skins and garments covered in moldering dust.

Soon enough it seemed that we had come upon some sort of carnage littering the passage as if a battle had occurred at our very feet and the former denizens of this place had been wiped out. The clothing left here was in tatters and the weapons had for the most part rusted and decayed so that when we touched them they crumbled to dust.

Wondering what could be taking Mr. Dunn so long to get back to us I suggested we go and get him, but Oramel said for us to go on.

From the state of the skeletons I could not tell if there were but two opposing forces or what manner discerned theses forces. We found another antechamber and here did Oramel agree that we should wait for Mr. Dunn while we looked about. Inside this room were scrolls that fell apart like ash at our touch. Some few more lead plates were intact however along with what looked to me like instruments of some cruel torture. I had a cold feeling here and felt wholly unwelcome.

Oramel poked around a few dusty bins and concluded that there was no treasure here either. We still had not heard from Mr. Dunn though he should have had more than twice the time to return to us.

I recommended we go back to the entrance or at least the mess area when Oramel said we had only just begun to explore and learn. We then heard a murmuring of voices, gibbering from the dense darkness.

At first we each assumed it would be Mr. Dunn returning but soon enough we could tell not only that it was not his voice, but that there were too many distinct voices as well.

I panicked and went silent, hardly breathing but Oramel replied that perhaps Major Powell had seen the futility of the river and had come back and discovered us through perhaps the ventilation shaft from our cook fire, and that would explain Mr. Dunn's rather long absence.

How I wanted to believe that, I hoped for that very answer, but alas I knew it could not be so because the voices were coming from the wrong direction of the tunnel.

I said as much to Oramel but he called me a fool saying it was but echoes in the dark.

The voices came closer and were mumbling in a language I knew not and they did fill me with such dread as I cannot fully write down. I backed away from the light of the lantern. The dark was so enveloping that I could see naught but my brother Oramel's face.

A force came whistling into the chamber and shocked my heart with its cruel sharp sound. I watched Oramel and he could no longer deny the presence of something so unseemly, so unholy that he daren't speak its name. He turned to face the darkness just out of my sight and I saw him clutch his chest and he wheeled to face me with such a look of horror as I have never before beheld. The horror. No words escaped his mouth but I saw the most wretched silent scream as even a veteran of the war of states has witnessed.

Oramel fell over dead and a wave of coldness hit me and the lantern went out.

WHISPERS OUT OF THE DUST — DAVID J. WEST

I felt skeletal fingertips wash over me and I fought their awful possession with everything I had as they clutched and tore at me. All the while chittering their horrid teeth and snatching bites of my flesh as I writhed through them like worm in carrion.

I don't know how, but I gained my feet and found the threshold of the chambers door to the tunnel and while I could see none of my attackers their bites and grasping's did not cease. Nor their vile mocking voices either.

I knew to go to the right and I struggled tripping over bones and dross, choking on the vapors of rust and decay.

My pursuers did not stop and several times I was knocked from my feet and bones pricked my flesh in lustful embrace.

I was near the end of my strength and willingness to escape, my voice had long since gone hoarse from the screams. At last a light was dimly received from up ahead.

Upon reaching the edge of light I saw that I was still only at the crossroads of the tunnels where the shrine to the tall mummy gods lay.

And horror, there upon the altar lay a butchered Mr. Dunn!

His clothing was shredded revealing numerous small wounds reminiscent of perhaps gigantic mosquito bites. His blood flowed lazily into the collection trough and there crouched behind and drinking from said trough was a skeletal lich of these forgotten peoples.

The thing paid me no heed but did succor itself from the crimson draught of my butchered friend.

Behind me I heard the clattering of bones and I knew more of these foul undead were coming.

I went to rush past the drinking fiend when it reared up and grabbed a hold of my wrist and this time I felt flesh rather than just bone. This thing was regaining its foul semblance of humanity! Flesh was returning to it as quickly as it had supped upon poor Mr. Dunn! And shock, it was resuming its former appearance, that of a dusky skinned woman with hair dark as a ravens wing.

I struck back and it lost its grip on me for a moment and I ran past to escape.

The clacking and clattering of bones was still upon my heels and I did not stop running until I reached the outside world.

The moon was high outside and the stars above gave weak comfort. I did fear that the night would allow a pursuit so I ran on in a foolhardy bid for life trying my best to sight a way up the canyon walls.

I thought I heard pursuit but could not be sure, I ran on so hard, and so afraid to look back and see what dark horde came after me.

Sometime by morning, I reached the top of the mesa and though I was gashed and bruised from a thousand wounds I kept moving if only to be away from that awful place. I still had my pack with pen and paper, and astonishingly my revolver though I had been too afraid to use it, but I had forgotten my canteen and was indeed suffering even by mid-morning.

I was incredibly relieved that nothing had followed me over the rim of the mesa. I travelled down what might have been either a game trail or an Indian path until I found a small village. I believed these Indians were Sheewits[21] Paiutes but I could not be sure.

___

[21] Shivwits.

I found that a young man among them could speak poor English and gave me some water. His name is Saw Bucks? And he did tell me what direction I might go to get to white civilization. I spent the rest of the day with them and they were indeed curious about my wounds but I did not yet feel like speaking about it.

I slept uneasily and was ready to head to St. George and the Mormons in the morning. But the Sheewits chief wanted me to stay another day and heal my wounds more, they told me that Saw Bucks would guide me in a day or so. I reluctantly agreed though I had wished to be farther away from that terrible cavern.

Come evening, I had packed my few possessions and felt good and full from the food the Sheewits did feed me. Saw Bucks could not speak good English but is a pleasant companion. I prepared for sleep when an uneasy feeling stole into camp.

A shadow wandered into the Sheewits camp and it seemed no one bore it any mind but me. It was a woman with a haggard dusky face wearing faded red clothing and what looked like canvas trousers. They looked familiar and I realized in horror as she approached that she was wearing Oramel's trousers. It was that unspeakable ghoul I had seen devouring Mr. Dunn's very lifeblood and her she was trailing me like a hound of death!

I drew forth my revolver and shot her dead until I had emptied the chamber. I was about to reload and keep firing when Saw Bucks and the other Sheewits tackled me and clubbed me unconscious.

Saw Bucks told me when I awoke the next day that I had murdered one of their tribe and I would have to die.

I tried to explain what had happened that she was no Indian but a ghoul, a lich from the cavern of doom.

Saw Bucks said that such was not possible that they [The Sheewits] did not speak of such things. It seemed they knew of the cave but considered it bad medicine and tried to deny its existence.

I begged Saw Bucks to let me write my last letter and that it might get to white men that he could have my pistol and other valuables. To this he reluctantly agreed and he is sitting with me here as I write this last account of my horrific ordeal.

They will slay me now saying I am a murderer, but know this, I only slew a demon in human form, if indeed it could even be killed for Saw Bucks told me that the body was dragged away in the night by coyotes, but he said this as if he was trying to talk himself into it. I suspect that they are shedding my blood as a way to appease these wretched old gods who do secretly hold power and sway over this enchanted land.

May there be a road for me in my passing.

Seneca Howland

Account of William Asa, September 1st 1869

I was delivered a letter from a Shivwit name of Saw Bucks with instructions that the man who had written it, wanted it given to Major Powell. I confess I did read it before taking it to Major Powell myself and was quite stunned at the contents, but I did steel myself to hand it over to him and act as if I did not know of what it said.

I did travel to the Majors camp and gave him the letter. I then waited as unobtrusively as I could to gauge his reaction. I spent a small bit of time speaking with Major Powell's men while sharing in watermelon grown at St. Thomas. The Major read it with some interest and after furrowing his brow and calling it terrible and impossible libel, he proceeded to throw it in the fire.

Snatching it[22] from the flames I was chased out of their camp with not but a few bruises and curses to my name, but I was not about to give up the terrifying message to the flames.

The next day when the major came to town, he demanded the letter. I did not relinquish it until the Major insisted to Bishop Leithead that it be surrendered as property belonging to the U.S. Government. I quickly made a copy, then gave Major Powell the original which I am sure he soon destroyed.

I have never forgotten this tale and I do often wonder about those evil and blood thirsty gods of the old lands that Seneca Howland spoke of. Do they still wander out in the wilds, do they still hunger for human blood and when might they call upon someone again in some forgotten and lonely place?

---

[22] That this incredible letter was ordered destroyed by John Wesley Powell can be of no doubt, the Major's order for its return was documented in several journals of the time. His motivations were quite clear and while he did declare the fate of the Howland Brothers and Mr. Dunn a libelous thing he did make peace with the Shivwits at a later date declaring the matter closed.

"But not all men seek rest and peace; some are born with the spirit of the storm in their blood."
— Robert E. Howard

Right Hand Man

Account written by George D. Watt[23] in January of 1870 and left in the possession of Daniel Bonelli[24] in St. Thomas.

We had only been in St. Thomas proper for but a few hours and already Brother Brigham's de facto and oft times drunken bodyguard, Orrin Porter Rockwell, was embroiled in the middle of quite a ruckus with the local red natives.

It seems that the Paiutes, who camp alongside the 'Big Ditch' – a canal that flows through St. Thomas to irrigate the fields therein, began to have a dispute over a woman. Supposedly one man decided to claim the wife of another man and the two began scrap over her and gradually a large number of the restless braves took sides.

They did have the civility to lay aside their weapons and duel using but their bodies until but one could claim victory and thus gain the woman. But of other such barbarities in

---

[23] George D Watt is notable for being the very first Saint baptized in England, after having won a footrace for the honor thereof.
[24] Both George D. Watt (head LDS Church stenographer and co-inventor of the Deseret Alphabet) and Daniel Bonelli were later excommunicated from the LDS Church for their affiliation with the Godbeite Movement. More on the Godbeites is covered in my novella *Fangs of the Dragon*.

the fight they had many, especially in the way they treated the squaw during the conflict.

She, unfortunately had no say in the matter, but such is the way of the savage. The two sides did beat each other furiously wrestling and boxing one another after a fashion and it did sway each way in an undefinable manner as far as I could perceive.

When they weren't beating each other over the head, they would then grab the woman by the arms and pull her each way in a veritable tug of war virtually killing the poor creature.

Now some of the Saints did try to intervene and thus save the woman but they were largely beat back by the strong willed natives whose blood was up in the heat of the moment. And of course Brother Rockwell's intervention was especially misconstrued as he has all the subtlety of a pair of brass knuckles.

He approached them when they were pulling hard on the young squaw and he admonished them to let her go and settle the dispute without harming her. They however took it to mean that he was saying he wished to join in the fight and he, being a white man, was the instant focus of their wild aggressions.

Rockwell suddenly had some twenty braves assaulting him and while for a moment one might have thought that the bearded gunslinger would be overwhelmed, Rockwell who has always been a hard man to handle, proved himself to be the meanest, toughest man I have ever seen.

I should add that at this point in the evening, Mr. Rockwell had already had a fair amount of drink in him and could not nearly have been at his full wits and capabilities.

At one point the braves had all taken hold of Rockwell by his arms and legs, picking up fully off of the ground and having him stretched out like a Christmas goose, but he ferociously kicked his legs until they were forced to drop him and he struck them with his fists until all tumbled down and then all at once he was punching them into submission. He whipped the lot of them and they did concede and allow him full access to the squaw. She herself was more than resigned to such a grim fate as that.

The braves having fully accepted that he was the victor, now cheered that the conflict was resolved and that he was the 'wyno'[25] Mormon.

Rockwell then did try and turn her over to that man whom he believed had the legitimate claim to her , but she did refuse such saying that he [Rockwell] was the man who had fairly won her hand and that she did belong with him now.

This put Rockwell in more of a fix that he had anticipated even facing off against twenty men. He told her he was already married and she only brought up the LDS custom of plural wives. Rockwell said that he did not wish to take her from her people and upset her family and that she should stay with her first husband.

To this she reluctantly agreed, though she said she was still truly his squaw and would only stay with her first husband on Rockwell's permission and that when he should desire her, she should come to him by and by.

She did also give him a small beaded medicine pouch she said she had made and placed sacred items inside. She said it was enchanted and would protect him from the great evil and ghosts he would soon encounter in this country.

---

[25] This is an amusing double entendre for Porter as, 'wyno' means good in Paiute, but also sounds like 'wino' in reference to Porters alcoholism.

Rockwell reluctantly put it around his neck, wearing it much to his apparent chagrin. But I must add that he did never take it off so long as we were in the Muddy Mission.

And so ended our first night in St. Thomas, which I must say ended up being the lightest conflict of the visit to the Muddy Mission.

Now Brother Brigham had asked Bishop Leithead to have a flat boat large enough for a wagon and team, prepared for the sake of going down river to do some exploring of the region. This was accomplished shortly before we arrived but upon inspection Brother Brigham seemed to have changed his mind and declined to float the river. This was obviously disheartening for those who had worked so hard on the project as timber was hard to come by here. But he did encourage the Saints there to remain and work hard in the region even if they should remain there forever.

That last particular remark is on account of the restructuring of the territory boundaries and that as of now the Federal government had moved the markers now making St. Thomas within the state of Nevada instead of the Utah territory, and as such the inhabitants were now a full three years behind the exceedingly high state tax commissions of Nevada. This did constitute quite a financial burden upon the folk as making a living in that arid land was already difficult enough.

These incredible hardships of living in this desolate land did make quite a few of the Saints wonder on their place in the kingdom and I can't say that I blame them.

I did have a long talk with Brother Daniel Bonelli on my own tribulations within the kingdom and with my recent reconnection after having been disfellowshipped on account of my adherence to the counsel of William Godbe. I cannot as yet say that I was wrong, but at this time neither will I say

I was right. The fate of the Godbeite reformation remains to be seen.

The flat boat did however see its use. The matter began on the next morning, when one of the Paiutes came to our camp and did call specifically for the help of Brother's Brigham and Rockwell.

Apparently the squaw Rockwell had rescued the night before had been taken by a bitter shaman by the name of Toohoo-emmi who was reputed to be quite evil and always working mischief in the area. He had slain the woman's husband and made some incredible demands that we all knew by no means would Brother Brigham abide by. This Toohoo-emmi was lord of a place known as Kai'Enepi or 'Demon Mountain'. The other Lamanites came to express similar grievances and soon enough the chiefs delivered their plea to Brother Brigham for help in dealing with the wicked shaman who was so vexing their lands and peoples.

At first it seemed that Brother Brigham would not hear their pleas as he had said they should sort this thing out themselves but this only caused confusion and much grumblings. It looked like things were going to get out of control and in an attempt to normalize relations with area bands, we did convene a meeting with Tut-se-gavits, chief of Santa Clara band; To-ish-obe, principal chief of the Muddy band; William, chief of the Colorado band; Farmer, chief of St. Thomas band; Frank, chief of Simondsville band; Rufus, chief of the Muddy Springs band above the California Road; and Thomas, chief of the band at the Narrows of the Muddy. Sixty-four braves from the seven bands accompanied the chiefs to the meeting. And this was one of the few times I saw Brother Brigham smoke the peace pipe with the Lamanites.

WHISPERS OUT OF THE DUST — DAVID J. WEST

To the overall request for assistance Brother Brigham replied that he would do what he could while also saying that they should still take care of their own problems. To-ish-be replied that while he agreed there should be a separation and such that this was a spiritual matter that was beyond his people's abilities and that we [meaning the Mormon brethren, who said we had the Great Spirits blessings in all things] should be obligated to do something about this wicked man who could consort with devils. This made Brother Brigham smile in a way he knew he had been caught with words. He agreed to send who he called his right hand man for just such a situation, Orrin Porter Rockwell. Brother Brigham said he would have Rockwell go out and solve the matter—if the Paiute would also put forward a squad of their own best men for the job and in this they very specifically volunteered a young medicine man whom the local saints called Chief John as well as five of their stoutest braves. Chief John was somewhat reluctant to accept this charge and I did understand that for some reason he was looked down upon, but until later I had no idea as to why.

And here is where I was also roped into accompanying this venture as Brother Brigham decided that I should go along and record their doings. It would be fair to wonder if he wasn't punishing me for the whole of the Godbeite debacle and I did wonder if this wasn't a surreptitious way of simply being rid of me should some unfortunate accident happen along the way. It is unkind of me to write or even think such things but this wretched land and heat has played with my very reason.

It was agreed that we should depart in the morning and that evening as I shared dinner with the Bonelli family I was told of some of the more sinister happenings in the area that were attributed to this Toohoo-emmi. He told me that the goings on in St. Thomas have been eerie as of late. That it is not meet to go out at night as strange things have been seen in the hills at night and some folk have been known to disappear. He said that the call of wolves has been terrible close and that he and others have taken to melting down silverware for the sake of keeping the pure metal as bullets close at hand. Brother Bonelli did give me a handful of the precious cartridges should I need them on this adventure.

We did have the good fortune of Chief John speaking good English as he would be our translator if needed along the way. Neither Rockwell nor I speaking Paiute with any proficiency. We took the afore mentioned flat boat down the river to gain entrance to Toohoo-emmi's abode. It was said he ruled from an ancient cliff palace that sat atop Kai'Enepi, the Demon Mountain. Our respective leaders bid that we should float downriver until we arriving at the trail leading to his mountain. Take the fight to him and force a resolution of some kind.

It was a pleasant enough trip down the river and Chief John did tell us a number of things about our antagonist. It seemed that this Toohoo-emmi, whose name meant 'The Black Hand', had once been the chief medicine man for the Paiutes but had recently been deposed since he began dabbling in black magic and being far too removed from the Great Spirit. He had been seen going into trances with his eyes only showing their whites and talking with unseen forces. All of this may very well have been fine except that firstly some animals [horses] had gone missing and then finally people started to go missing and it was assumed that Toohoo-emmi was sacrificing them after the manner of the Old Ones.

Chief John was the one who had exposed this horrible crime and was then made medicine man for the tribes. This was a dubious honor because he had not been trying to take that position but merely right the wrongs that had been done. He had at first expected to exonerate Toohoo-emmi of the wild rumors and accusations but instead found indisputable evidence to condemn him. This certainly put a strain on things as I understood they had been quite close at some time.

Rockwell was rather indifferent toward all of this, spending a lot of his time using his saddle as a pillow and drinking Valley-Tan, letting his hand trail lazily in the warm river. He expressed no interest in Chief John's tale and I felt it would be up to me to make peace once we found Toohoo-emmi and had the maiden returned. I hoped that by expressing Brother Brigham's annoyance at this behavior we could peaceably conclude the matter. I should have recognized Chief John's worry earlier on but I was ignorant of such things then.

It is true that sometimes we become blind to our own world outlook and standing, we can become complacent and forget outside views and I have stood in that place far too many times.

We had travelled some distance downriver when Chef John pointed out we were being followed and I was horrified to find out by whom or what he meant.

A trio of great black snakes swam in the river pursuing us. They dipped their heads every now and again and when they did I saw their scaly tails twist in the water a good ten paces behind where their head had been, I estimated these reptiles to be in excess of twenty feet long!

I woke Rockwell and asked him to look and be wary. He casually took a drink of his whiskey and blinking, answered that it was but beavers, and true these heads were near as large as or even larger than a beavers head, but I assure you, they were indeed snakes of enormous size.

Chief John explained these serpents were servants of the Toohoo-emmi and would protect his domain from the likes of us. I took hold of a paddle as I had no gun and I again urged Rockwell to take up arms against this impending threat. He laughed and said there were no such snakes so large nor in this part of the desert. Granted, he did use much more colorful language than I shall repeat here.

The other five braves were in a panic, crying out "Nooyooadu!"[26] But they did utilize their bows and rifles to prepare for the coming assault.

The serpents made a swift reconnoiter of us aboard the flat boat and did strike almost simultaneously panicking the horses into breaking their tethers and flinging themselves off the flat boat and into the river and very nearly cap-sizing us in the process. I regret that it took such dire action to bring Rockwell's attention to our situation.

Rockwell was up in a flash and had his snub-nosed Navy Colts firing like the devil's own cannons, and I must admit I did wonder about a house divided against itself. It seemed that for now the devil did protect his own as the snakes dodged his bullets and ducked back under the waters no harm done to them but we had lost all of our horses and one of the braves already.

Then the snakes did launch themselves at us once again. I did batter one of them with a paddle dazing it, I suspect for it dropped back down into the murky waters but it certainly was not yet deceased.

---

[26] Paiute for 'Snake'.

WHISPERS OUT OF THE DUST — DAVID J. WEST

One brave shot a pair of arrows into a serpent and it remained sluggish though it did not halt its attack. Another brave was knocked off the flat boat but Chief John managed to sink his tomahawk into the sluggish one's head slaying it, though in its convulsion it hit him in the chest and fell back into the river.

Rockwell watched swinging his pistols whichever direction he did look and it saved him, as one snake reared from the waters suddenly and was met with both barrels full into the mouth. This blasted beast also slid back into the river with a splash of gore across the flat boat. I tried to remain steadfast in the face of such horrific violence and felt it was near beyond me.

With but one serpent left, we all kept vigil and also did rescue the one brave who had been knocked into the waters. We had absolutely lost the horses as they did not rise from the surface and we did suspect the serpents had grabbed their legs and drowned them along with the first brave who was knocked overboard.

There was some swirling in the murky brown waters but nothing came of it but our own fears.

When the final serpent did not attack, Chief John said he suspected that it had been Toohoo-emmi himself and that without help the wicked shaman would not attack as fierce a foe as we few again by himself, and that Toohoo-emmi had many other resources to fight and wear us down including other black magic's that did bring much fear into the braves though I am quite sure that it was not his intent to worry them.

Chief John said we were floating nearer to the abode of Toohoo-emmi and bid us be watchful.

We floated to a spot in the river where a small canyon opened giving us but a very narrow view like unto a doorway to another realm. Beyond the cliff walls we saw in the distance some verdant greenery while a small reddish stream flowed into the Virgin River. I expressed some surprise that this stream and canyon were not on the maps that had been supplied me by either George Brimhall or Anson Call[27] but then neither did they mark a map with any place known as Kai'Enepi either. As near as I could understand Chief John's explanation, he seemed to be trying to find the English words to tell us there was a 'glamour' over this place and that what was once a sacred place of the Paiutes was now polluted and held in thrall by this Toohoo-emmi and his wicked band.

Rockwell guided the flat boat into the sandy beach area of the canyon and we did ground the vessel and pull it as far onto shore as we could muster now lacking the horses. We staked and roped it to some boulders though it would be no small feat for someone else to come along and dislodge it, even perhaps a large wake of the river could do the deed, but we were resolved to continue on despite the potential loss. None of us thought leaving a lone man behind to guard the flat boat was a worthwhile venture in this dangerous country.

We had not gone far beyond the shoreline when we found two dead men. One had his head blasted away by gunshots and the other had no head, as if cleaved by a tomahawk. Two arrow wounds were also in his backside. It took my getting some used to the idea but Chief John insisted these two men had been changelings or shape shifters and were in actuality the serpents we had so recently encountered. This was the wildest explanation I had ever

---

[27] Two of the original LDS explorers of the area.

heard but I could not deny the bloody truth at my feet as much as I truly wished I could.

Porter was silent at this revelation, but neither did he say it was as impossible as I had first pronounced.

We hiked along the narrow cliff walls always with an eye to the sky above which gave us but a sliver of light in this dark canyon. Thrice rocks tumbled from somewhere far above nearly braining us in the process. Chief John said this was the work of the Nimerigar, or little people. He said they were cannibals and allied with Toohoo-emmi. Again I scoffed but felt a grim fear well up in my breast as I thought I saw some dark child dash behind a boulder. Sure that my eyes were playing tricks on me or that perhaps I had seen a child rather than a tiny man I expressed as much to Chief John who bid we prepare for an attack.

Rockwell spit out a curse and I told him to remember who we were and what we represented and he looked at me with those deep killers' eyes and I found myself unable to continue speaking.

A shrill high-pitched cry echoed from the cliffs and the sharp twanging of bows announced the attack of the vicious Nimerigar. Tiny arrows filled the clearing before us and the miniscule shafts caught one of our braves in the knee. He had time but to shout in terrible searing pain and then he passed away while convulsing and foaming at the mouth like a mad beast.

Poison! A treachery most foul! Chief John warned us to avoid even a scratch from the deadly missiles. The tiny needle like armaments bounced and ricocheted from the boulders about us and soon enough it was clear that the diminutive assassins were flanking us as our cover from the storm diminished.

Porter cursed again and said something to the effect of having enough and he would test his mettle here and now.

He stepped out into the barrage and yet, none of the cursed darts struck him, it was as if he bore the wake of a great airship before him and the missiles did swirl out and around him on a peculiar breeze, such could not be said of his bullets though—as he took aim at the Nimerigar and shot a score of them before they fled in terror.

Rockwell even captured one, who was no larger than a babe in arms, though fully grown according to Chief John. The little man had an ugly head that was quite large by comparison though all of his tools, clothing and moccasins and the like were similar in fashion to the Paiutes, though just the size for a doll. I should add that he had wretched teeth and did spit and hiss furiously as Rockwell held him by the nape of the neck.

Chief John was quite taken aback but did proceed to try and question the Nimerigar, who as Chief John later told us had never before been captured by any man, let alone a white man to whom they were usually invisible.

Bitter though he was, the Nimerigar, whose name he said was Pu'wihi, said he and his war party were to defend against the enemies of Toohoo-emmi, as he was now their true Lord and master.

I sensed that I was witness to the dying of a race that would soon be no more, as I understood some small amount of the exchange between Chief John and Pu'wihi that there were no longer any women left to the Nimerigar and that it made Chief John sad though they were his ancestral enemies. I felt I was uniquely disposed to feel that pain, as that very loss and decay is a part of my own religion and belief.

Bargaining with Pu'wihi seemed to make little headway but finally we were able to work an exchange of the tiny man showing us the traps his people had left on the trail balanced upon our word that we should no more harm his folk if they too left us alone. To this he agreed and he then did call out a sharp cat-like cry and yipping that was met some miles down the canyon and we saw no more of the tiny people. We did however keep Pu'wihi a prisoner accorded good treatment. His curious presence was unnerving to me.

We made camp for the night against an overhang in the rock, that would not allow any enemy to sneak up behind us and even gave good cover should enemies try and shoot at us.

Rockwell said he did not like the place but it was getting dark and there was no way to get the braves to continue on with us in the gloom. Not that I wanted to myself as this was a truly dark and frightful place. Strange calls filled the night and even Pu'wihi said he did not know all the creatures that made such awful cries.

Chief John blessed our spot and bid we always keep two men on vigil all night to ward against any evil dreams that might befall us.

I found it a hard place to go to sleep as the sandstone was both hard and cold and the eerie feeling of doom hung upon me thicker than my wet blanket. But sleep I did for some time in the early hours Rockwell shook me awake saying to hold onto something solid and try to get to the highest point beneath the overhang.

I was confused and groggy with sleep but I heard an awful roaring that filled me with such terror, I wondered at what wretched demon was tearing down the canyon toward us with the speed of a locomotive. It must have been a giant for I heard the snapping and twisting tree trunks shattered at its very passage and I wondered aloud how we could possibly fight this devil.

Rockwell answered there was no fighting it, we should simply weather it out in the high ground.

I did not understand, but he had been so very nonchalant about all of our trials and now as a giant was thundering toward us he simply moved to the upper edge of the hollow and grabbed hold of a boulder. I shouted at him over the approaching din, that perhaps no bullet or blade could harm him but what was I to do against this new foe and who I asked was it?

Flash flood was his taciturn reply, and then a mowing demon of crunching twisted roots, brambles and tree branches' turned end over end pushed by deep brown waters. We were all huddled up against the far side of the overlook as the scraping hands of the wood and water monster pawed at us, spit in our faces and took hold.

One of the braves was stuck through the gut and carried away into the morass, churned, chewed and swallowed before he could even scream. Pu'wihi had leapt onto Chief John's shoulders and was the highest among us, not that it was entirely safe. Brambles crashed among us and clawed deep gouges in the stone and our flesh.

Then it got worse. I heard an even deeper sound of cracking stone as hairline fractures above our very heads spread like black lightning.

This is Toohoo-emmi's black magic at work, shouted Chief John.

What could we do? Be crushed by a hundred tons of rock above us or eaten alive by the flash flood below?

You a praying man? asked Rockwell, better pray now, he said over the thunder.

WHISPERS OUT OF THE DUST — DAVID J. WEST

We all did pray in whatever tongue was ours at birth. The cracks in the stone above our heads grew in size and the flood did not cease in intensity. I was praying with all my might and yet I did doubt that I would come thru this crushing predicament.

The waters were still churning like a death roll but what should fling itself at us but a massive log. Rockwell and Chief John each instantly seized hold of the upturned thing and jammed it against our roof.

The other braves helped and we all did hold it steady against the great load bearing down upon our collective heads.

The grating force of thundering doom did not cease but the mighty trunk held but a few moments longer.

Pu'wihi cried aloud saying the waters were receding and in truth they were. Rockwell cried that we all had to dive into the waters despite the torrent and make for just upstream as he gauged the cliff above us would fall the other direction. It meant trying to go against the current but that would be our only escape.

We dived into the dark muddy waters and I instantly felt dragged away. It took all my strength to simply stop being pulled downstream. I caught a hand and felt myself yanked toward the far side. One of the braves had a handhold in stone and was pulling me toward him.

Rockwell was the last to jump away just as the trunk was snapped like a match stick against the stupendous crumbling cliff face. I couldn't see for the splashing water and freed dust behind. I thought him surely dead.

Chief John and Pu'wihi had made it to the upper edge and called for the rest of us to make it to them.

The brave and I struggled but made it to waters only a couple feet deep and we trudged on, albeit on the opposite side of the torrent. It was then I realized I had lost every single possession I had brought with me. Even my shoes were stolen by the river in flood.

Calling out, we found that we had only lost that gutted brave and Rockwell. We gathered about a small rocky knob and tried to start a fire. There were now only Chief John, Pu'wihi, myself and three braves. I wanted to be happy I had lived but given the circumstances I was now hit with incredible despair. Surely this wicked man Toohoo-emmi would come for us now that we were beaten, disheveled and largely unarmed in his canyon. The wave of fear and anxious trepidation was staggering.

Then Rockwell burst from the waters like the Kraken himself. His eyes glowed fiercely and I did not doubt any longer that he meant to kill this Toohoo-emmi and he was surely the man to do it.

Rockwell still had one of his pistols although he said his ammunition was soaked and may or may not be any good. He also had his bowie knife. One of the braves still had a spear, another a bow with a few arrows and Chief John had a knife. It was a pitiful armory for what we meant to do but there was no turning back now.

Chief John explained that the sudden wave of despair I felt was more of Toohoo-emmi's black magic and that I should resolve to will it away the next time it came. I wanted to believe that as strange as it may sound to those of a rational thought process, as I did not wish to admit that I could be responsible for my own melancholy arrest, but alas I did think it was likely my own self and not some black magician casting it at me from the great beyond. Too often that blanket of misery has rested upon my shoulders and caused sleepless night and gloomy days. I should overcome such but it is a road one must walk alone.

By the time the weak fire had almost dried us, it was near morning. Faint glows gathered in the crack of sky above and we felt as if we might have a moment of peace. But Chief John said he thought that Toohoo-emmi would send men down the canyon after us in an effort to sweep thru after the flash flood in the likelihood we would be weak and disoriented. I asked that if he had sent that wave of despair out like a cloud over us, did he not know we yet lived?

He said yes, he knows at least a few of us live but how many he could not be sure. He also said that Rockwell's life force may have given the impression that we had greater numbers than we truly had and we should be wary of a great force coming.

Rockwell laughed at that and said he liked those odds.

I was not amused and took to finding stones I might use in a sling, which I fashioned myself from a torn shirt sleeve.

The other unarmed brave also hunted for something he might use as a weapon while Pu'wihi said he knew where a cache of weapons were though they were not for our size. We said we should gladly take them all the same.

He had us follow him upriver just a short quarter mile until we came to a small side canyon, we could not fit thru the entrance but Pu'wihi quickly disappeared thru it. I did doubt we would see the diminutive big-headed man again but he did return with a few of his peoples spears which were almost the size of regular man's atlatl. I gladly accepted three of them as well as a tiny obsidian knife. The other braves received the same as I, but Rockwell was not interested in such primitive weapons. He took to rolling his ammunition in his hand hoping the powder was dry and complaining that he had lost his whiskey while I had no shoes!

The day had broken and we heard forces echoing down the canyon walls. Chief John said it sounded like at least a dozen men, surely the shock troops of this terrible magician. We made as ready as we could in a fork, where we thought it would be best to ambush them and strike first, hard and fast. It was not gentlemanly by any means what we planned to do but these are desperate seasons.

It was more than a dozen men, perhaps two dozen. And as I steeled myself to cast one of the atlatls in my hand, Chief John cried out, not in outrage or the call of the warrior but in joy. These were his friends and compatriot tribesman from further afield come to join us in the good fight.

They spoke quickly but with some enthusiasm. It seemed that some brave rafting downriver soon after us came across the dead snakes and went back and spoke of our victory. This so heartened the chiefs that braves were eager to join our cause whereas earlier the few who had come were indeed brave souls fully expecting to be killed in the struggle. There were some words I could not follow for the sake of the two men who had died, Two-Sheep and Antler Head. But now we had a veritable army to bring Toohoo-emmi to task.

Rockwell was also quite pleased as they gave him some of their stores of ammunition and one of the braves had an extra pair of moccasins for me which meant the world in the sandy rocky ground.

We forged ahead up the canyon, I couldn't help but hum my favorite tune by Sabine Baring-Gould[28] upon our march. This was indeed a glorious day and we would triumph I was sure of it now!

---

[28] Sabine Baring-Gould wrote both the Werewolf Book - the definitive collection of werewolf and vampire lore and 'Onward Christian Soldiers' which is likely what fellow Englishman, George D. Watt was referencing.

We did not have to go more than a few miles to where the canyon widened somewhat allowing a fuller view of the sky. Here the canyon walls were incredibly high as black things circled far above.

Chief John pointed out Kai'Enepi and the cliff palace of Toohoo-emmi above and we did marvel at its ominous face. It was near the top of a sheer mesa, small black windows stood out from the angled towers of red gold stone and I found myself thinking that it looked like the eyes of a three headed predatory raptor. In all my wildest dreams I never saw such a cruel edifice and did wonder again at the circumstances of my place here.

Rockwell alone was undaunted, spouting such raw words of American courage as I did doubt the Paiutes save Chief John even understood though they did acknowledge the spirit of his good intent and were ready to follow him up the spine of sharp rock to the terrible cliff palace.

Here Pu'wihi said he must leave us for he could not engage in this open rebellion of his Lord's people, but he did whisper that he hoped for our success and that if we should survive, he would be grateful as it would mean the dark lord's mastery over his people must be ended. He seemed to express some trepidation in such being possible.

Rockwell urged him to tell his people to join us and fight back against this common foe, but the Paiutes were indeed skittish at this suggestion having always regarded the Nimerigar as their sworn racial enemy. I could readily tell that the diminutive man regarded them in the same light.

Pu'wihi said he would speak with his elders but to expect no such help from his broken people that they were few in number and he did not know if even he might be shunned for his association now.

Fair enough, said Rockwell.

High above we could see dark shapes of men moving about the citadel and we did wonder at their numbers and resolve. Surely there must be more of us, but it would be a far climb to the summit and even then we should be wearied and worn. The angle up looked to be quite steep and had just enough slant that a man might walk or crawl with his hands, but should he slip or tumble I did not think anything would stop him until he should hit the ground, and of that end, I am sure that man would be no more.

We prayed as a group and some of the Paiutes did sing their death song. Some smeared colored mud upon their bodies and hair and in so doing they looked positively monstrous, appearing more like golems of mud and clay than men of flesh.

We all drank our fill of water and did fill our skins. Rockwell and Chief John did set us to go up the cliff face but to have some small amount of distance between the men so that if one should be shot with arrows and fall and roll he should not force the rest of us to tumble after. Also they had it in mind that a wave of our fighters might be able to loose arrows while one group advanced, then the other would cover them while the other climbed higher. In such a way we might minimize our possible casualties and save lives. I must say I was surprised at both Rockwell and the savage's tactical sense. It was wholly unexpected.

Rockwell led the foremost group while Chief John should lead the second. I was with the second as I had no gun nor was I of any real experience with a bow or spear. I just hoped to find a useful means of assistance somewhere along the way.

Rockwell became the point of the spear going forward and did find his way about some jagged boulders and did warn others coming behind of loose stone and what he perceived might be traps or purposeful rock slide spots.

The long haired gunfighter of a saint had gone past a few of these hoolies[29] when a catamount leapt upon a man right behind him, tearing the poor brave to pieces before Rockwell and the others shot it to death.

It was indeed suspicious and quite unnerving to the men. It was also curious that the beast had not attacked Rockwell who should have been the first to disturb it, passing within only a few feet of its now visible bone strewn lair.

That was when Chief John pointed out Rockwell's medicine pouch that he still wore given him by the squaw he had won. She had said it would protect him and now it seemed that it assuredly had come to pass. I now wondered after his previous encounters with the great serpents, the Nimerigar, the flash flood and now the mad catamount.

Rockwell laughed it off, but neither would he remove the enchanted piece of leather and bead work either. He urged us on to the cliff palace, though to be wary of more traps.

We were perhaps half way up the summit and in an area where there were no more large boulders for anything to hide behind, nor for us to receive any cover should the still absent enemies above shoot at us. As I came to this realization is when their missiles did fly toward us.

Both stones and arrows came now from some height above us within the cliff palace, though I rarely caught a glimpse of our assailants for I was dodging the threat.

A rock the size of a man's head took the head of a brave beside me and his body went tumbling after.

---

[29] Local vernacular for a large boulder.

Rockwell shouted that we should charge their placements as best we could keeping a steady stream of fire to keep their heads down and aim off.

This was exceedingly difficult for both the terrain which was almost sheer, the lack of rifles and the perilous assault from above.

I could not hope to cast one of my atlatls at this range and had to trust to the others to keep such a retaliation strong. I saw Rockwell hit several of the men at the top of the parapet and city, for I saw them fall from its front and land upon some flat surface at the base of the cliff palace's walls.

From somewhere yet farther on within the cliff palace, we all heard a strange dirging horn blast thrice and almost all of the Paiutes now shook with terror for the sound was indeed answered by cries from some infernal beasts farther upon the slopes. The Paiutes cried aloud saying that it was the Eaters from the Sky and even Chief John was unnerved at this terrible revelation.

Rockwell however had closed a good distance to the cliff palace and was well ahead of any other man. He still fired his guns in rapid succession and every few shots I saw another one of the defenders fall or cry out. If it were not for his reckless stalwart behavior I do not believe any of us would have left that mountain alive. This at least renewed the Paiutes courage enough that they did heed Chief John and rush up the slanting face despite their fears, which were not unwarranted.

The strange cries echoed from the canyon walls and I heard such an awful report as I hope to never hear again. It bounced from the cliff face behind, above and below. It was disorienting and I could not tell from which direction the monstrous call began.

Then they were upon us.

WHISPERS OUT OF THE DUST — DAVID J. WEST

Hideous monster birds of a greater size than I would have ever thought possible. Like denizens of some lost world these reptile looking avian's swooped and clawed and grasped at us and only now was I grateful for the atlatl scar for it saved me twice from their clutches. Others were not so lucky. I saw a brave grasped about the shoulders by those sharp talons and carried high above only to be dashed against the rocks. The foul monster birds then dove and took chunks of his flesh squawking at one another only to take flight again and try the same upon another poor soul.

We now faced two fronts, the tumbling rocks and arrows from the cliff palace above and the monster birds that swooped at our exposed backsides.

I managed to look up at the cliff palace in time to see Rockwell ascending the first level and shooting men who came at him with clubs and spears. At least the barrage from above would ease a moment.

The enemy blew upon the horn again and I heard his cry as Rockwell sent him spilling over the side of the palace walls to crush his skull amongst the jagged stone.

Chief John shot one of the monster birds and this seemed to allay the fears of the Paiutes who fought back with renewed vigor and more of the monster birds wheeled from the skies with mortal wounds until there were no more.

We dashed up the face to reach the pinnacle city all the while ready to clash with our assailants. Oh how my blood pumped through my veins at this wild cataclysmic battle. Never in all my dreams had such a confrontation occurred as when we met the savage painted men that awaited us at the top.

I relate herein that some of this was a bloody daze to me as I was struck once with a glancing blow on the head from a war-club but I did feel my spear pierce the foe and I know

I drove the weapons point home in his breast until he expired. Men died all around me whether my comrades or the dark painted enemy I could not fully tell for the din was so very loud and the blood, oh the blood that washed over this fell tower! Sounds of Rockwell's guns blazed somewhere above and I made my way toward the sharp serenade of black powder.

Then Chief John was at my side and bid me follow him as he had a rifle and we went up ladders from one level to another. Cyclopean stone towers met us at every turn and in some few were dark things waiting, relics of a bygone eras when wicked men held sway over this land and always the trail of blood from Rockwell's fearsome talent was left apparent at his recent passage.

I began to fully understand and appreciate Brother Brigham's words that Rockwell was indeed his 'Right Hand Man' in such matters as these, though I would not believe it if I were not living them myself.

In our journey through the cliff palace we did find a chamber of slaves that had been stashed away by their foul masters. These poor souls were gaunt, sick and feeble; they were afraid that we meant them harm, but Chief John assured them we were there to help and he did enquire of them the whereabouts of Toohoo-emmi and his most powerful acolytes.

They told us that the above mesa had a terrible kiva and that entrance was forbidden to only but the most trusted men of Toohoo-emmi. Were the slaves to dare approach, they were pitched off the cliff. The slave then said that if we had attacked the cliff palace then surely Toohoo-emmi and his men had retreated above to their sorcerous refuge.

Out upon the level stage overlooking the whole of the canyon, I could just make out a veritable ladder of a path with handholds cut into the living rock and as I scanned all the way to the top I saw Rockwell disappear over the edge. I told Chief John and we did prepare ourselves to follow.

Chief John called to the Paiute braves and three of them joined us on the ascension. I was last in line as I held less skill in the climb and was the slowest amongst us. Halfway up the dizzying height and I realized I bore no weapons either but I would not stop now.

Clinging to the holds I made my way over the edge to look upon the horror of the kiva's entrance. I was aware of the existence of these underground chambers and their sacred use to Indian rituals and practice, but I had never yet beheld one for myself and this was not what I had expected. A dark rectangular entrance loomed ahead and I could not help but notice the resemblance to a skull's mouth, as the mound loomed up and two dark, what would could only be described as eyeholes, were spaced evenly farther up. The aura coming from it gave me chills and though it was full daylight, all seemed dark and foreboding here.

I wondered that I should be so alarmed, as this was the longest space yet where I had not heard Rockwell's guns and I wondered if he yet lived.

Chief John leveled his rifle and bid the three braves accompany him forward into the entrance. I was close behind and as I took a step inside, cold wind met my face and a terrible smell of stale blood and offal met my senses threatening to catapult my morning's nourishment free. Chief John and the braves went down the ladder and I followed.

Pillars of light from the skull's eyeholes above pierced the dark but the rest was lost in shadow.

We are not alone, whispered Chief John.

Nothing was in sight and I moved forward a step but was quickly pulled back by Chief John as something struck right where I had been. I felt the air and heard the thump.

We surely disappointed the ambush by not dying.

I saw the quick movement of black on black only because of the sheen of sweat glinting faintly upon the muscular giant who charged me.

Then the flash of guns lit the gloom and a cry of shock and pain revealed we had lost a man. Framed against the gunshots I saw big shadows of men charge and soon I was struck across the mouth by a broad hand and taken to the dirt floor. Chief John's rifle blasted a man and I felt a body fall against me on the ground. I struck back against who I know not. And then just as suddenly it was over.

Breathing heavily I was picked up and brushed off. Chief John's voice said we had slain the men who meant to ambush us and that we should go outside to the cliff behind the kiva where he believed Toohoo-emmi and Rockwell had gone as everything inside the kiva had been but a trap or distraction.

I was dazed and bleeding from a scalp wound but I followed and realized we had lost two of the braves who had come with us but Chief John was resolved to hurry and deal with this wicked threat.

Outside and behind the skull like mound of the kiva stood Rockwell, facing a tall man covered in black paint who held a woman to his chest with an obsidian dagger to her throat. He called out in broken English for us to surrender to him and he would spare the woman.

Rockwell answered, Like Hell. He had his pistol trained on the man but did not pull the trigger as he did not wish for the man to pitch her over the side if he was hit. Let her go! Rockwell ordered.

WHISPERS OUT OF THE DUST — DAVID J. WEST

Toohoo-emmi knew he was in a desperate situation, his men were all dead and we had conquered his sacred city. He had nothing left but a hostage and a glass knife. His terrible eyes swept back and forth at us and he muttered some wicked verse low under his breath.

What foul powers of darkness can be contained in but mere words I know not, but I was a witness that they do take hold and demand to be reckoned with. The Paiute brave who had followed us all the way up the slopes and fought beside us suddenly went mad and tackled Rockwell sending them both off the precipice.

Toohoo-emmi threw the woman at Chief John and lunged with his knife. I was in shock but grasped the woman and pulled her from between them. She was either in shock or drugged as she went limp in my arms and went to the ground.

Chief John grappled with Toohoo-emmi and I went to assist him when I heard Rockwell's cry for help.

He was not dead?

Clinging to the edge of the cliff with both hands, the long haired gunfighter had the possessed brave holding at his left foot and growling like a mad dog.

I'm trying to shake him loose but I can't do that and climb up, shouted Rockwell.

I looked behind me and Toohoo-emmi and Chief John were in a terrible tussle. I looked to Rockwell and he shouted, Hurry up and do something!

I picked up a stone the size a fist and looked from Toohoo-emmi to Rockwell and his assailant.

Rockwell saw what was on my mind and said, don't miss!

The mad brave was trying to bite Rockwell's slipping boot and I carefully released the stone and hit the poor deranged man square in the face. He swatted at the missile and came loose of Rockwell and plummeted the hundreds of feet to the ground below, all the while clawing at the air as if he might suddenly take flight.

I extended a hand to help Rockwell up when I felt someone tugging at my shoulders to send me over the brink!

Toohoo-emmi had knocked Chief John senseless and was striving to eliminate me! The last of his foes still at the summit.

I pushed back in vain, Toohoo-emmi was much the stronger and I had no traction.

Watt! Duck!

I looked just in time to see Rockwell training his pistol right at me. I ducked and I felt the heat, powder and air cascade as the bullet went right past my ear. I was deaf in it for days. But Rockwell had sent a slug right into Toohoo-emmi's face. Yet the wicked shaman was not dead!

He gargled and grasped at his face as blood poured over his black-painted body, his cheek and ear were ruined but he was not yet even close to dead. He turned and ran from us as I pulled Rockwell up and over the edge.

Chief John had been sorely struck but was still alive as well. The woman remained catatonic but appeared otherwise undamaged.

I helped Chief John to his feet and senses as Rockwell went in pursuit of the foe.

Toohoo-emmi had run to back side of the mesa and to another ladder and further down a relative back way to Kai'Enepi. As near as I could tell, from this high place you could climb down into another slot canyon and eventually make your way back to the Virgin River.

Rockwell was already halfway down went Toohoo-emmi reached the bottom and began kicking and knocking away at the long ladder in an effort to knock Rockwell loose.

He succeeded in knocking the ladder loose and it started to fall over to the left and into an awful gorge. Rockwell leapt free and caught a jutting pinnacle of stone.

Toohoo-emmi then disappeared into the crags and we saw him no more. It took Rockwell sometime to be able to climb back to our position.

We would camp in the cliff palace that night and care for our dead and wounded. Chief John led us all in prayer to cleanse this place and among the purifications that were done, we did burn some of the towers and the great skull kiva at the summit. It was a bonfire for the ages and finally by morning did the thing collapse upon itself and release what evil spirits it held.

The next day we began the long arduous journey back to St. Thomas and Rockwell did grumble exceedingly about, 'the one that got away'.

Chief John reminded him that we should see Toohoo-emmi again soon enough and though it was a bitter defeat for him, the black magic medicine man would not leave us alone for long. He would have to be challenged again.

We reached St. Thomas a day later and I did then begin to relate the events to President Young and herein record them for myself alone as it was not recommended that we share such foul sorcery with the body of the Saints.

* * *

The last night we remained in St. Thomas, there was a dance and gathering of the Saints. President Young did advise them to be sober minded and such but it did not dampen the festivities much. I was discussing some of the recent political maneuverings with you [Mr. Bonelli] and as you may recall I was called away by a Brother Sorenson.

WHISPERS OUT OF THE DUST — DAVID J. WEST

Now I shall relate the rest of the evening to you and leave this full recollection in your care as I cannot take it back to Salt Lake and further scrutiny.

I was told that on the southernmost edge of St. Thomas there was a ruckus of some kind. Some said that it was not unlike the one the first night we had arrived and that it was involving the Paiutes. Still I was advised to go as I had some doings with them in the days previous and it was thought that perhaps I could help in calming things down.

I arrived to discover that Brother Rockwell was already there and was facing off with a rather large Paiute. Who to my astonished eyes turned out to be Toohoo-emmi himself. He spoke in an angry broken English, calling down blood and fire upon Rockwell for the destruction of his city and his acolytes. That he did blame both Rockwell and Chief John for the desecration of his sacred priesthood and he was there for terrible revenge and through the power of Xuthaloggua [his toad-like idol] he would conquer.

Chief John had not been found as yet but Rockwell did not seem worried. He said to the big Paiute to, throw down and do his worst.

Toohoo-emmi then raised his hand which held the curious idol and crying aloud the earth rumbled and rose at his very feet.

I was aghast at the sight of it.

In a circle of some twenty feet round, the ground churned and pitched as if boiling and then a blast of lightning went from his hand that held the idol of Xuthaloggua, to Rockwell, centering upon the medicine pouch from the Paiute maiden that he still wore.

While the lightning from the toad did seem intense it was swallowed whole by the medicine pouch and no harm came to Rockwell.

WHISPERS OUT OF THE DUST — DAVID J. WEST

Whatever force there was blasting from the vile shaman, it was taken and held by that maidens pouch. Rockwell looked askance at the blackened pouch and then to Toohoo-emmi and he said dryly, My Turn. He drew his snub-nosed Navy colts and emptied both barrels he into the dark shaman.

There was no effect at the impact of those slugs. The dark man smiled mockingly and proclaimed the power of Xuthaloggua and I could see that even Rockwell was worried a moment.

But as Toohoo-emmi went to attempt a second blast from his idol, the Paiute squaw who Rockwell had rescued twice over, struck the toad-like deity Xuthaloggua, with a broad stick.

The wicked shaman did wince in fear as the broken clay god crumbled in his hands from the sundering. He then grabbed the squaw and stabbed her with his dagger.

Rockwell shot again and this time blood flew from the shaman's chest.

I counted at least nine direct hits in the big man's torso as he shook with the force of them and then fell over dead with a look of astonishment upon his face.

The maiden was dead and for her Rockwell did mourn.

But those who had gathered cheered and swept over to Rockwell and then some cast stones at Toohoo-emmi's corpse and even his destroyed idol. Before I could say anything, Rockwell admonished them to stop and bury the wicked man's body right where it lay, especially since the ground was already broken up and made for easy diggings.

After this was done, Chief John arrived and asked about what had happened. He looked to the medicine pouch Rockwell had and proclaimed that it had done what it was intended and was now used up. That seemed to strike Rockwell fine and he cast it off.

Chief John was also rather concerned on where Toohoo-emmi was buried and he was shown approximately where that was. But because the ground had been thrown up in such force it was difficult to tell exactly where the body lay so a guess was ventured forth to tell Chief John and he then went and fetched a sacred palm tree which he did plant on the spot that most agreed was correct.

I thought it a strange custom but he assured me that it was necessary. He said that unless great care was taken it would be possible for as powerful a sorcerer as Toohoo-emmi to rise again from the clutch of death unless his dark spirit was contained by the sacred tree.

I had seen the broken shattered body full of bullet wounds and my rational mind thought that his diabolical resurrection impossible yet, I had seen many terrible wonders that week previous including the lightning from Xuthaloggua and upheaval of the earth at his command so I cannot be sure how many more dark and mysterious wonders are in our world, hidden away in some terrible corner of the globe, defying, Nay! Even mocking our imagination and comfort in the world at what is both right and sane.

Rockwell and Chief John and I did take the maidens body farther out into the desert and did give her a sacred funeral pyre, which we alone did witness.

I leave this record with you my friend, that in case such information is ever needed again it will be at your fingertips to be put to good use.

Until then, farewell.

Walking among the sacred palms in the Moapa Valley, near St. Thomas.

Above: Looking westward from the hills near the ruins of St. Thomas

Below: Someone has been 'Casting the Runes' upon a sacred palm.

"Whenever I take up a newspaper, I seem to see Ghosts gliding between the lines. There must be Ghosts all the country over, as thick as the sand of the sea.... We are, one and all, so pitifully afraid of the light."
— Henrik Ibsen

The Thing in the Root Cellar

Account of Isaac Jennings by Ace Perkins[30]: January 26th 1875

With the Mormons moving out of Moapa Valley, Isaac Jennings had made quite the haul of selling off the lumber from their homes and acquiring the harvest from their fields which he purchased from them on promissory notes. Yes sir, he had made quite the deal considering his reparations would amount to little more than the cost of the seed they had been originally purchased for. And let's not even get into the fact that he never did pay back one dime from those promissory notes either.

Never one to look a gift horse in the mouth, Jennings had done very well for himself all things considered. He harvested the wheat and had a ready market thanks to the Paiute Indian Agency and he even had the Paiute doing the work of harvesting for cheap! Yes sir, everything was looking quite all right for Mr. Jennings that is until he had something decide to call his root cellar its home.

---

[30] Ace Perkins was a Paiute orphan who had been raised and taught some basic schooling with the local Mormon children. After the Mormon exodus he stayed on in St. Thomas to be near his people.

WHISPERS OUT OF THE DUST — DAVID J. WEST

It all started when one of the more favored [on account of I could read and write] Ute work boys, by the name of Ace (that's me) went to put some canned peaches down there.

I had a good armload and then also a case of pickled beans made by Mrs. Jennings. I went down the stone steps and I unlatched the door which a big lock on account of Mr. Jennings didn't want none of the Paiutes to steal his stores, they had been won't to do that often enough. I only had the key for a short spell and only when he knows it was me that had it. Only took me a half second to know something wasn't right.

It smelled wrong, it felt wrong and the hair on the back of my neck stuck out like it was the cold of winter night and I was about to be swallowed by the dark.

I heard a rasping of some kind and a shuffle in the dark like to think something was rushing right toward me, but I couldn't see nothing coming and yet even in the darkness I could see the jars of peaches and fruit on shelves at my eye level all the way to the back, but still I knew something was coming. I shut the door fast as I could even though I dropped and broke the jars all over the stone steps.

And I had shut it just in time too for something slammed against that door and I was up those stairs and away before anything else might happen to me.

I hurried and went and found Mr. Jennings and told him about it. After he was done a swearing at me and telling me what a fool I was he went to go look for himself.

WHISPERS OUT OF THE DUST — DAVID J. WEST

Going with Mr. Jennings was his favorite hand, a big buck of a Paiute name of Charlie Three Toes[31]. I followed a short ways behind sure that I would be exonerated when they found whatever was in there.

I honestly didn't know what it could be, but what I did know was that it had a wicked bad aura about it, I knew it was there soon as I opened the door, though I never saw anything. I decided it must be a ghost since there had been plenty bad stories about ghost and evil spirits around here. It had to be that, especially since I didn't see anything, but boy did it slam against that door.

Well Mr. Jennings, he held a lantern and Charlie Three Toes held a shovel and they mocked me once again looking at the broken glass and peaches and beans on the stone steps. Mr. Jennings said he was gonna take that outta my pay and I knew that would be an awful lot of work. But I hoped it would be forgot soon as they experienced the ghost for themselves. I held my breath just a waiting for them to get a taste of that horrid spook.

They opened the door just a tad at first, then a little more, but nothing happened. Charlie Three Toes opened it all the way and stepped in and still nothing. Mr. Jennings he went in and swung his lantern around and said, "See, nothing! You little fool. You're going to pay for those jars and peaches and I'm going to charge you top dollar for them too!"

I asked if they didn't smell that awful reek and they each in turn said it was nonsense that's just how root cellars smell this time of year when it gets musty and damp. I looked all

---

[31] The Paiute Charlie Three Toes was called that on account of having cut off two of his own toes with a shovel once when he was drunk.

about and sure enough, I didn't feel that terrible presence no more, it was surely gone. I looked at the hard packed ground and there were no tracks, no sign of anything having been there and that's when I was sure as could be that it was a ghost had been there.

Being mighty nervous to go back alone, I took to make excuses and being busy with other work but by and by Mrs. Jennings got wise to me and sent me with another crate of canned beets to go into the root cellar.

I in no wise wanted to go it alone and managed to convince Hailey Summers, a girl from my schooling who happened to be walking past, to go with me. She was a year older than me and liked to act it too but we were still friends. I didn't bother to mention the ghost, I just told her there was something I wanted to show her in the root cellar. She smiled big and followed me.

I fumbled with the keys and couldn't do it on my own so I had to put the crate down. Hailey laughed a little and said to let her give it a try. I said no I could manage and then turned the lock and slowly let the door creep open. I was waiting for any sign of that spook when suddenly Hailey took my hand, pulled me into the root cellar and kissed me.

I was not expecting that.

I liked it for sure but couldn't let go of that hint of worry about the spook being in the root cellar. Just then we heard that weird loud rasping, like a coughing fit or other and we just looked at each other and I told her to run and get out. I heard something coming but again I couldn't see nothing. Just as I got the door closed it was pushing and stamping at the door with a good force. Then it stopped.

Hailey up and slapped me. Said it was mighty cruel of me and my friends to scare her and take advantage of her, that I shouldn't have spooked her into stealing a kiss like that, and again that ladies don't do that kind of thing. I said I was sorry before I knew what I was saying sorry for and she stormed off before I could even say that I had no friends a spooking her in the root cellar that this was a for real ghost. But she was gone and the crate of beets was still outside the door.

I knocked on the door and the spook started battering at it again and there was no way I was gonna open up to him. I did wonder at why he being a spook couldn't just come thru the door but I guess I was also grateful that he couldn't. I supposed that it had to be a spook since he was plum invisible and maybe a curse had been put on him being trapped in there on account of some bad things he had done in life. I had heard about another bad witchy man being trapped somewhere under a sacred palm once before.

I decided I would go and get Charlie Three Toes and show him the thing rapping on the door. It took me a little while longer than it should have to find him and he was mad about it but came with me anyhow to check on the root cellar because I was so insistent and sometimes he likes me to read to him.

At the door I knocked, hoping the ghost would respond in kind and start hitting the door again. But nothing happened. I told Charlie Three Toes that he had to believe me that the spook was surely there but just a tormenting me alone. He didn't seem convinced but I told him it had scared the daylights out of Hailey Summers too and she ran away. That didn't go no way in convincing him either but he said we best put the beets away.

We opened the door and slowly looked in. I swear it had that bad stink to it but Charlie never could sell anything. I put the case away and told Charlie he had better come and check again with me sometime if he wanted me to read to him again.

By the time I got back inside to do more chores Mrs. Jennings was powerful upset saying I was one of the laziest boys she ever did see. I tried to explain to her my predicament with the root cellar and she called me about all the names that Mr. Jennings already had too, but her way was just a little more spiteful.

I went home wondering if I would even have a job the next day and a part of me figured it wouldn't matter none, I shouldn't have to deal with folks that talked like that or with their spooks.

Sure enough come daybreak, Charlie Three Toes told me I wasn't wanted at the Jennings place that they didn't need my kind of help. I know he was sorry to tell me but still it stung.

Without work or school for the day I went down to the Muddy and decided I would try and catch some fish. I spent the better part of the afternoon there and caught a few of the big carp that I would take home to Mama Louise to cook. I decided to sun myself on a good sandy spot along the river and I left my dead fish in a small pool beside me tied up with string. I soon fall asleep and had some good dreams.

I woke up at near sundown and was astonished that someone would steal my fish right out from under me. I had tied the fish together with stout cord through the gills and the whole caboodle was gone! I figured it had to be one of three boys I knew but then I saw something in the sand. A weird track of some kind that wavered across the ground through and left a peculiar toed print with claws. It was big as a man's foot and I wondered what kind of man left such a print and would steal fish. I decided it was that damned spook, because none of those boys could have snuck up on me so quiet like, it had to be the ghost.

I tried to follow the track but lost them in the grass. Of course it was heading back toward the Jennings place too!

I went home hungry that night determined that next time I would not fall asleep after catching fish.

Come the next day, Charlie Three Toes told me I was supposed to come to work. I was surprised but got up and went with him to the Jennings place. Mr. Jennings gave me another verbal beat down about responsibility and duty to the ranch and whole lot of other things I didn't feel applied to me. Mrs. Jennings railed on how I had left them in a bind and that there was now more things than ever to clear out of the kitchen and put away in the root cellar.

I truly wondered if I shouldn't quit for good.

I did however start carrying cases of jars out to the root cellar. When I got there what did that old ghost do to taunt me? But leave my fish heads and the cords on the stone steps. That mean old joker of a ghost was a taunting me more! They was covered in some kind of bile but there was no doubt it was my very own fish. I looked around a little more for some other sign but I didn't see anything. I was mighty irritated though.

I went to open the root cellar door, thinking soon as I do this that spook is gonna rush me, but this time soon as I touched the key to the lock the spook he started thumping and slamming up against the door. That was enough for me, my young heart can't take this no more. I went and told Mrs. Jennings that I cannot handle this ghostly business and she had to fire me or give me a different job.

She slapped me upside the head and told me what a lazy cuss I was and that she would show me there weren't any such things as spooks.

WHISPERS OUT OF THE DUST — DAVID J. WEST

I followed her out to root cellar thinking either this ghost is gonna take her or me. I wasn't exactly pleased about either outcome. I tried to show her the fish heads and cord covered in bile but she was too busy berating me to listen. She took the key from my hand with a jerk and unlocked the door. There was no sound or movement just yet. She gave me the severest of stink eye and then picked up the case of beets and went inside.

I waited an awful long minute expecting screams as Mrs. Jennings finished putting her stores away and then called me to come in and put away what I was holding. I did so and wondered mightily on why the spook wasn't showing himself now.

Nothing, now I was sure that spook was tormenting but me alone. Later I found myself busy with plenty of other chores around the house and it weren't til late that I was tasked with again gong out toward the root cellar. Evening made me uneasy in passing by and I was alarmed when what should I see but the Jennings dog, General Beauregard lying amongst the shrubs on the far side of the root cellar. I called to him but he did not come when I called. Though he seemed to be lying there and shaking a bit.

I stepped closer thinking him ill when he stopped moving and something went bumbling through the shrubs.

General Beauregard was no more. Something had given him a terrible bite. There was a wide half-moon of neatly impressed teeth marks across him. It was such a strange bite, all net like the teeth were small and the bite was so big, I didn't know what could have done it except that spook trying to give me the willies and I must say he did. I ran back to the house as fast as my legs could carry me and fetched Charlie Three Toes and Mr. Jennings. I told them what I saw and they rushed out.

102

WHISPERS OUT OF THE DUST — DAVID J. WEST

We reached the edge of the shrubs it having only been a minute or two and General Beauregard was gone. We didn't see no trace of blood either. I swore I was telling the whole truth but Mr. Jennings he cursed me again and said he wasn't about done with my crying wolf all the time. I said it wasn't no wolf but he just said I was a simpleton.

He said when General Beauregard showed himself again in the morning it would prove me a liar. But I saw the bite on that dogs fore quarters and I don't think I'm gonna see him again.

Next day I took more canning to the root cellar but this time I was ever watchful outside by the shrubs too but I didn't see anything. I knocked upon the door and there was no sound. I noisily unlocked the door and slowed creaked it open. Nothing happened, so I quickly put away the case and shut the door. I was glad I didn't have to go back all day neither.

Later that evening when I was walking back to my place I saw Hailey Summers again. She asked me if I had seen little Tommy Turner. I said I hadn't but she told me he had been missing since early that morning and she was helping look for him. I joined in the hunt but we didn't find any sign of him by midnight. Some people suspected he drowned and went down the river but I had to wonder if the spook was behind it and what it might do next.

The next day Mrs. Jennings had me run another case out to the root cellar and before I even got to the door, the thing was banging against it. I ran and got Mrs. Jennings, I wanted her to see what the spook was doing.

She rolled her eyes at me but proceeded to storm out to the root cellar with a new case of beets. We got there and the spook had gone quiet again. She unlocked the door and went inside after calling me all sorts of choice names.

WHISPERS OUT OF THE DUST — DAVID J. WEST

I stood outside thinking I should probably ought to just quit and see if I could get work in Overton or St. Joseph when Mrs. Jennings, she screamed like banshee.

She dropped the case of beets, I heard them crash in a thunder, and she came a running out screaming she had seen the face of the devil.

She slammed the door behind her but didn't drop the bar, the spook he started thumping against the door and it was cracking open a couple inches with every push of his might.

I rushed to help hold the door and as I came down the steps, I saw the spook through the cracks. He must have been a dead man for his skin was black and red and scaly dead looking. He was a rasping and panting at the door but I couldn't make out no words.

We finally dropped the bolt and it held good and he couldn't come out. Only then did she pay attention to my fish heads a few steps away. She agreed that even the devil might devour human food at times and that this surely was his work and he must be tormenting them [The Jennings] on account of their sinful ways[32]. I didn't doubt the possibility of that answer I just wondered why it had to involve me and my fish in any way. And what about General Beauregard and now I'm inclined to think Timmy Turner too!

Well Mrs. Jennings she went and had me fetch Mr. Jennings and Charlie Three Toes and they came in a huff and demanding just what had happened. When she told him about the thing in the root cellar he laughed at her and called her nonsensical and said it was all just old wives tales and stupid children that believed such rot.

---

[32] Ace clearly sympathized with the swindled Mormons.

She glowered at him insisting that it was the truth and the devil was a punishing them for their thieving ways. She declared she had seen the face of the devil that he has a jagged toothy smile and that he had beady black eyes and a red and black face that was tattooed like.

Even I didn't know what to make of that, but I had seen the spooks skin and wondered if the dead were rising from their graves. What if the root cellar was built upon someone's grave? It was dug pretty new only a month or two old, and I supposed such a thing was possible.

Well Mr. Jennings he looked at me, Mrs. Jennings and Charlie Three Toes and he knew he would never hear the end of it if he didn't open that door and face the devil.

So he took a deep breath, had a shovel in one hand and Charlie Three Toes behind him with a pick ax and he throwed open the door.

Nothing. There was nothing, no sound, nothing standing there or anything. Mrs. Jennings started to cry and Charlie Three Toes was trying to keep from laughing.

Mr. Jennings he yelled that this was all my fault that I had told enough lies to upset the whole community and that he didn't never want to see my face again and that he was gonna see to it that I never came around again after he gave me such a licking.

Something grunted at that.

Mr. Jennings he looked from me to Charlie Three Toes to Mrs. Jennings and back to me and it was plain that none of us had made that strange eerie noise.

He went back to saying he was gonna tan my hide but stopped real abrupt.

Right about then we all heard that same horrible rasping and I looked knowing full well that that spook was gonna be rushing toward us. I looked at eye level not seeing nothing but then the shambling sound kicked a case low and I saw just a foot or so off the ground the biggest Gila monster in all of creation!

The thing was long as a man and rasping and charging.

I backed away quick but the beast bit full down on Mr. Jennings and shook itself trying to turn upside down it seemed to me.

It was hard to hear on account of Mr. Jennings crying out and Mrs. Jennings terrified screams. Charlie Three Toes he had jumped something fierce and run off. It was left up to me.

I took the shovel Charlie Three Toes had left and started battering down on that giant lizard. Nothing seemed to make much effect on him so instead of hitting him with the flat of the shovel I took to trying at piercing him with the shovel blade. The beast had flipped himself upside down as the lizards are wont to do[§] and I hit him square with the shovel a cutting somewhat into its throat like.

It wouldn't let go of Mr. Jennings, not even as I took its head clean off with multiple strikes of the shovel.

Well Charlie Three Toes he come back with a scattergun and he shot the monster in the belly and that took it all apart. We each then had to get a crow bar and pry its dead head off'n the leg of Mr. Jennings who was caterwauling something fierce.

It took some doing but we finally managed to get that monsters jaw loose and get Mr. Jennings free of its awful bite.

[§] Gila monsters only have venom in the bottom jaw which opposite of venomous snakes with the poison fangs in the top of the jaw. Gila's will then sometimes flip their prey upside down to better let gravity assist in poisoning their prey.

We rushed him into the house and got a poultice on his leg while Charlie Three Toes then went and fetched the Doctor from over in Rioville.

I went back and looked in the root cellar now and poking around found a smallish tunnel that the monster must've been using to come in and out of. I also found a clutch of eggs.

I felt bad about killing that big wonder of the world. I also felt mighty silly at thinking that it was a spook. I filled in the tunnel which emerged out by the shrubs where General Beauregard had been lying. I suspect the good old dog had seen the monster and they got into a tussle and the dog he lost. I wondered if'n Mr. Jennings might lose his battle with the Gila's tooth venom but weren't much bothered at the thought of it.

I took the clutch of eggs out of the root cellar and gave them to Chief John for safe keeping. He said he would take them across the river and up into the hills. That the big lizard spirit of the desert would live on where they wouldn't harm our people.

It weren't long after this that Mr. Jennings, he lived but was what you would call real frail and sickly like. Also seems a lot of the money double dealing had back fired on him lately and he said he had to be moving on. He would send for Mrs. Jennings in the by and by and he left near a broken man. Least that's what I told them reporters that asked from up in Salt Lake[84].

I did stay on and help out on the farm and let me tell you, Mrs. Jennings was awful polite to me from then on.

---

[84] Deseret News remarked on Mr. Jennings legacy in its January 26th issue, 1875.

"The murdered do haunt their murderers,"

— Emily Bronte

Black Jack's Last Ride

The sworn solemn testament of Dan Brill: June 27th 1876

"I am a wicked man and know that tonight I am truly at the end of my earthly rope. I ask not for forgiveness nor pity just perhaps someone to believe what I do hereby record as my last will and testament. It is the Gods own truth and my life blood will seal its veracity.

I met up with Black Jack Reed and rode with him and his men[13] for nearly nine months. In all that time we shot and killed ten men, held up seven coaches, rustled cattle, stole horses and hit the bank in St. George once.

Lastly we did also waylay and kill one more man for whom we were well paid though I never did know who he was nor who was paying Black Jack for the job. He was awful quiet about it and I did suspect at first that it was a prominent man whom we did not want the Mormons to pursue us for. Black Jack did say one night before we did the deed, when he had a lot to drink that it wasn't the first time he had been a part of such a thing and his soul was already damned for murder anyhow, so he might as well be paid for it.

---

[13] Black Jack's gang at this time consisted of himself-Jack Reed, Dan Brill, Shan Balden, and a man known as Siebrecht.

Having long been on the wrong side of law and order myself I ain't much of one to judge, I've robbed and murdered but Black Jack did seem particularly plagued with bad dreams and chronic pain these last few months on account of the evil things he had done. He kept a stiff upper lip as most Englishman are won't to do but his was driven by a bitterness and resentment only the truly desperate and wicked attain.

Black Jack often had horrid scabby sores upon his legs and could not ride as long as he had when we first met. He would wash his legs in the ditch that ran through the lower St. Thomas fields, and I was always careful to drink upstream of his condition.

I repeat myself sometimes because I am a relatively unlearned man and find it necessary to go over again what happened in my mind to make sense of it. Our last job was the murder and again I stress between myself and my Maker that I did not know who it was to be.

Black Jack had the four of us ride out halfway to St. George along the Virgin River and wait a good long time. I think he knew what kind of dire condition he was in so he had given plenty of time for us to rest and for him to soothe his infected legs in the cool waters. I suspect that he had been given word of a time and place of our intendeds crossing and we had but to wait in the shadows of a narrow gulch within the canyon. It was cool and gave us much relief from the usual heat of the season.

We did let several wagons pass by without their being aware of our presence for the course of three days. Black Jack would watch them closely and once he was sure it was not our man lay back down and rub salve on his legs that he had received from a Mrs. Jennings.

We ate hard tack and jerky as Reed said we were to have no fire and not alert no one of our presence.

Finally come evening on that third day and we heard horses a coming down the Virgin River Gorge from St. George way.

A man was walking leading four pale horses. He looked to be a tall finely built fellow who stood proud and handsome guiding his mounts. He wore no hat and I was surprised on account of the heat and sun outside the canyon walls.

"It's him," cried Black Jack, "It can't be, but it's him!"

Jack looked pale and quite shaken but we took it as our order and we opened fire with great abandon as we had felt so cooped up and with itchy trigger fingers for the last of these three days.

Amidst the thunder of guns and storm clouds of powder smoke we all saw the man go down into the river, crying out, 'Oh Lord, My God!' as he vanished. His mounts bucked and galloped back down the gorge surely leaving the dead man lying in the river with multiple grievous wounds.

The three of us approached the spot in the river where the man must have gone down. Black Jack strangely hung back, gobs of sweat bleeding over his brow.

The distance had not been much, perhaps but fifty yards but already there was no trace of the man, the body was gone and there was no blood in the water. Even the horse's prints had been washed clean away by the river.

He must have washed down already suggested Shan and I was inclined to agree but Siebrecht shook his head saying the current was not near strong enough to float a body especially out of sight that fast.

I was inclined to agree with him also but there was no other explanation. The gathering darkness may have helped hide the body but the three of us were at least in agreement that no man could have survived the volley that we did give.

Black Jack was in panic and could not be consoled. We had planned to ride out of the canyon and put some distance between us and the murder but he was seated and rubbing his legs which now oozed worse than ever.

Of who the man had been he would give no answer. We waited only a short while and forcibly put Reed upon his horse and started down the gorge.

He cried out in pain at his legs many a time and we did our best to shut out the agony of despair that echoed from his lips.

We had just reached the open valley out of the Gorge when behind us in the dim star-flecked twilight we saw a rider leading three spectral mounts approaching with great speed. He was not dark as he should have appeared but instead was a ghostly white as his garments were glowing and hanging from him like a death shroud and his ghostly horses matched same.

I don't need to tell you this put the fear of god into us and we rode at all possible speed away.

We passed by the Joshua tree forest and did wait a moment to gain a breather for own horses and shoot this awful foe, but as we saw him come over the crest of the hill his specter of presence made me lose all courage and I remounted my horse and did away with Black Jack at my side clinging to his saddle like a man possessed.

Siebrecht stood fast and I heard him shoot his sharps rifle twice, but then it went silent and of him I never saw again.

Shan Balden caught up to us fast screaming that the ghost rider had taken Siebrecht's very soul! And he did note that now there were but three ghostly mounts instead of four.

WHISPERS OUT OF THE DUST — DAVID J. WEST

We raced through Mesquite without stopping sure that the rider was yet coming up fast behind us upon his relentless chargers. Galloping like that all night we did and as dawns light was about to crest the mountains I looked back and saw that our spectral pursuer was gone.

I was filled both with relief and anguish. I asked Black Jack again and again who the rider was and who had put the bounty upon his head, but of answers he gave none.

Upon reaching St. Thomas we brought together our resources and were oh so wary. I set a boy to keep watch for strangers and none did come into town all that day.

Black Jack went to Mother Jennings and had her change the dressings upon his sore legs. We then went back to our camp and took up some much needed rest.

When the thick hot night came, we sat by our slow burning cook fire and wondered at our collective experience. We spoke but little and I knew that we had not seen the last of our haunted foe.

Sometime after midnight when the coiling's of the fire winded down leaving only lackluster coals, the moon came out and put ghostly light upon all it touched, bathing the town in a sea of ashen grey. We waited a breathless moment and my ears stung at the sound of hoof prints hitting the hard packed earth.

Watching in every direction, I was in a daze at where the sounds came from. Black Jack moaned in a fitful state and I was not sure if it was from pain or from fear.

Shan Balden who was afraid of no man, stood up from the fire and looked at the road.

I saw nothing but it seemed Shan did.

The sound of hoof beats rapidly approached and Shan turned to look at me, then back to the empty road saying I'm next, then he fell over dead.

I heard hoof beats race away, but of that gruesome specter I saw nothing.

Black Jack shivered and drank and shivered and drank.

With dawn we two buried poor old Shan Balden and it was a wonder that a man who had lived as he had should have no mark upon him in death. We spoke few words at his graveside and put him in the ground with a small cross marked R.I.P.—S.B. to comfort his lost soul.

By noon Jack was caterwauling at the pain and his dressings were soaked in blood and pus. I had to carry him over to Mother Jennings. Mrs. Perkins was there as I brought Jack in and she begged her pardon but wished to remain. She asked Jack if he felt he was improving, to which he replied ""No lady, I am getting no better, at times the pain eases a little but I will never get well and for a reason, lady, I was in the mob that killed the Mormon Prophet Joseph Smith in Carthage Jail and every man who was in the mob has suffered just such as I am suffering, by the flesh being eaten off their bones by worms."

I saw the worms in his flesh and the oozing sores and it was truly a horrific sight.

We took the blood money we had been paid and did have the best supper we could possibly acquire in St. Thomas town, but once it was spread before us we did ponder on it and found we had no appetite any longer. Black Jack then smiled and said it was now for our hosts and with his best regards. They did thank us but I know they wondered at our grim repose.

We instead drank and Jack told me alone who had paid him for that wicked ambush he had planned. "I was at the crossroads of St. Thomas, Las Vegas, Pioche and Rioville when who should appear but Old Scratch himself. He told me that he had one last job for me and that t'was due. That

I was to ambush a man in the Virgin River Gorge and would know him when I saw him. He gave me this blood money of which I shall never spend and in my pain and fury I did accept his cruel charge."

We drank a bit more and Black Jack he laughed until he cried. He took out a worm from his mangled legs and showed me its mealy head saying, "Look here, this is the true measure of me. I am but a conqueror worm."

I then fell to a fitful sleep, where demons, goblins, and ghosts danced upon my grave.

I awoke to Jack cursing softly as he spilled coffee. To his credit he did offer me the last cup.

Thanking him I did wonder aloud if perhaps we should be spared this night as it was well past the witching hour. Jack gave a grim laugh and said he already heard the hooves of hell approaching.

Silence mocked my ears as the moonlight did the same to my sight, but the shivers running up my back sensed what the others could not.

I waited and listening hard again heard the ghostly tramp of a pair of hoof beats though I saw no one there.

Black Jack, he smiled at what he alone could see and said, "I'm as ready as I'll ever be."

He then expired in his bedroll and I heard the hooves of death ride away and swift to the west as Black Jack made his last ride.

I myself much to my shame did pass out cold in fright and wondering at my own marked and wicked name.

In the morning Black Jack's corpse was littered with worms, large black-headed maggots that writhed through his bones, and made his flesh fell apart. The men who saw him became sick and could not bear to look upon him any longer and we prepared a spot right where he lay. The stink was enough to make a butcher gag. With no other recourse we rolled him in his own tent canvas and buried him in an unmarked grave. He had no ceremony, no kindly words of the gospel or hope for the hereafter. For no man who saw it wished to recall that awful sight of his death mask again.

I finish this statement as evening comes on. I have nothing left to confess or say as I fully expect that after midnight that last hell horse will come a galloping in to drag me to hell and where I belong."

"Everything is not jes zaclky as it wus when u hurd from thes quarters afore. We hav been mad down hear, and one Piute got stabed in the back, and several Lamenites[36] had jes a little too much firewater fur thur good. An one Gentile wus mity mad, but he didn't hurt enybody by it. U understand now that Sant Tomas is not a town of the past any longer. No sur, she kumin to the frunt, she iz."

— Pioche Weekly Record: October 14, 1882

A Rose for Miss Dolly

The tale of Louis Fontaine as recorded by Jake Longabough[37]: November 7th 1882

This tale is old as time and reminds of many a legend of loves lost that few knew, but sit a spell and have a listen for I swear tis true.

There I was in the saloon having drinks with the boys and playing along with greasy cards when we done run out of whiskey and everybody had lost all their money to that shark from Pioche[38].

The saloon actually had a grandfather clock and when that thing chimed midnight I couldn't have believed how fast

---

[36] This unfortunate writer is sadly showing himself to Mormon.
[37] Jacob Longabough late of St. Thomas clearly thought himself a cowboy poet with this rendition of the tale of his friend and would be spouse.
[38] Almost certainly William Tinsdale a renowned gambler and card shark who frequented the area.

they all disappeared when it came time to pay up and buy someone else a drink for a change.

Witching hour somebody claimed and the others said that had to get some rest for church in the morning, pack of hypocrites! Some few folks were asleep at the table and some upon the floor, even the barkeep was up and gone or passed out or the like and I found myself in a terribly quiet establishment when all I could hear aside from snoring was a wee little gal crying.

Dressed all in white and lace and such and I thought I never did see such a sad but pretty little thing as her. The smell of lilacs permeated the room and I wondered for having only ever smelt them before near a tomb.

I looked her over and said hello, she blushed and then went to hiding her face. As I said she was a pretty little thing and I couldn't imagine what could be making her cry. I asked her, excuse me miss but whatever could be the matter?

She explained that her love was lost and she was dead, tired and all alone in the world now and couldn't find happiness til he came home to her.

I explained in my likely drunken way that t'was natural to feel that way sometimes but love is like the dawn and will rise again. She smiled at that and did ask if I had any other homespun wisdom to impart.

I liked that smile and I called her a rose and she said her name was Dolly and I did propose that she get to know me much better. That my name was Louis Fontaine but she could call me Lou. She said it back to me and Lord that was nice.

We did talk and laugh for some time I told her of all the places I've been from St. Louis for which I'm named and new Orleans where the dancing girls in red tutu's made me ashamed, up west to the Black Hills and the cold northern plains where the Injuns did give Custer such pains[39], I've been to Texas and New Mexico and even San Francisco but I never did see such a pretty rose as my miss Dolly.

She told me she has never been much of anywhere just here and there and expects that alone she won't be going to any place but despair. I asked her not to cry and said I'd be true and stay with you if you'll just not let any more tears fall.

She smiled at that and said she'd hold me to my very word and I'd stay most any place from now on with her. And as I spoke and thought I start to saw the dawn rise faintly from far behind the horizon she said it was beyond time to go, that she had a fine time with me and would see me soon enough and when my back was turned she was gone like the last stars of night.

I told the boys that I was in love that I'd met Dolly kind of and they did spoke that there was no such woman and no such gal last night in the poke.

Now some did laugh and some did frown and I guessed it was all because I was the one who had won her heart and interest hands down. But my good friend Jake, he said I'd had too much to drink and needed to sleep it off, give it some time to think, that I wasn't about to start no affair of any kind with this sweet little dove. They said I'd been seeing things and all that rot, that nobody else saw her while I sat on a cot.

Now I grumbled it's true and asked what do I do? She was the one for me that's sure and true. I couldn't have them discouraging me no more, no how. They cajoled and argued

---

[39] Custer met his fate at the Little Big Horn only six years earlier.

and swindled and shouted and near everyone said it had gone on way too far.

Who was she I pleaded, a married woman, a scarlet lady, a tattooed whore? I couldn't take their jokes anymore. What could I do what more could I say? To get them to see things just my way? Because love won't stand behind any closed door and soon enough I'd be asking for more.

The boys they bought me a drink and forced it down and then granted me another and another til I was ready to drown.

They took me down to the old churchyard that day and showed me the forgotten grave of one, Dolly Shauntay[a]. I left a single rose for Miss Dolly on her tomb I'd be joining here soon enough and there was room

I dropped my complaints and accusations galore for I knew that I should only have here about one day more. I spent my money upon my friends and gave them the best going away party I knew how to send and left them these words to leave all on the mend.. Come morning I knew I wouldn't be waking up in this world again.

Cause when the death angel calls, you best be prepared and with friends and the good Lord always be squared.[b]

---

[a] *"Sleep, Dolly, Sleep. Where flowers bloom and zephyrs sigh, Where I may come to shed the tear that streams unbid from sorrowing eye."* Those were the words upon Dolly's tombstone. No one knows who etched them or paid for the stone as she had no known family.

[b] Louis Fontaine (passed away from causes unknown) and was buried in the St. Thomas cemetery on Nov. 8th right beside a Dolly Shauntay, who had been laid to rest there the preceding year to the day.

"The [dangers] are the black rattle snake, the scorpion or tarantula, the centipede, a vicious, deadly reptile, and large green worms that come up from the ground."
— George W. Brimhall 1865

If I Call to the Pit[42]

The curious account of one Tom Dabney[43]: 1888

Tom Dabney's grandfather left England and Tom's father left Connecticut and Tom—well, he left St. George. It wasn't really that far to be leaving his father's house, but it did give him more than a good day's ride away from his mother's apron strings.

He joked that he came to St. Thomas because it was named for him. But he would admit to friends that it was to prove he could do something on his own and here in such a barren dead land he could make something of himself all on his own. He hoped. After all he had few enough skills but he had a quick enough mind when he applied himself.

Tom had just enough seed money to get a small plot of land that was richly irrigated by the Muddy River and the ramshackle remains of a cabin/adobe hut full of whiskey bottles and rotten deer hides. He had his doubts anyone had lived in the place before him, rather than just using it as a

---

[42] Job 17:14
[43] This tale is almost certainly apocryphal though Thomas Dabney was known throughout the county as a successful farmer and had more than nine daughters.

trash heap. It took some doing to clean the place up but once it was done and he had reroofed it, he was quite proud of the accomplishment. It was the hardest thing he had ever done before. Granted he had not had a very hard life.

Soon enough he was plowing the fields and preparing for a crop of radishes, carrots, onions and a few melons. He had picked these in part because they were what he liked and what he had heard was in demand at the markets in the territories. Tom had pitiful enough knowledge of farming but went into it with gusto and a belief that it couldn't really be that hard.

The heat in the valley was primal and it beat on him something fierce even for a youth raised in St. George. He found that he could fill his canteen with coffee beans and water in the morning, hang it on a tree and have a fine hot brew by noon[44].

Tom also discovered that watering his carrots too late in the day caused them to boil and die in the ground. This was going to be much harder than he had anticipated[45].

Forced to re-plow and replant a vast section of his fields, he began to ponder the wisdom of his choices in giving it a go on his own. An unscheduled arrival and visit from his mother cemented his resolve at continuing the sweltering ordeal and he borrowed from her to start over.

This time however he resolved to actually learn what he could from those he understood were the true masters of growing in this oven of an environment, the Paiutes.

---

[44] Prior to current standards and especially social outlook, coffee was a very common drink with the LDS pioneers.
[45] This was a regular occurrence for farmers in St. Thomas in the summer months.

Tom asked around and went to the in town dwellings of the Paiutes over by the Big Ditch[a] and asked about what grew best in the sunbaked condition of his soil. He heard a variety of answers and felt as if he was getting nowhere in useful solutions.

Then he found an old man in a bleached pair of canvas trousers with a turkey carcass around his neck, mutilated feathers dangled from his hair and dark coal dust smeared about his eyes. The old Indian had a particularly sinister look but this did not daunt Tom who was sure this man would have some ideas.

"Your ground is no good, it needs help to recover itself," the old man told him. "You need to call upon the earth spirits for help."

"And just how do I go about that?"

"I will help you, for a price."

"How much?" Tom asked, with some fair amount f trepidation.

"Not how much now, but later."

"What?" Tom scratched his head sure now that the old man was crazy as jack rabbit with heat stroke.

"Someday I will come and you will give me your daughter, your first born daughter."

"Heh, I ain't even married," said Tom, with a laugh, "how do you expect to collect on such a thing? Could be years. What if I never marry, what if I only have sons?"

"Important thing I help your crops grow now, you pay me when is time," said the old man, with a wicked grin.

---

[a] The Paiute day laborers camped along the Big Ditch as to be close to their field work. In the off season they went back to the hills and canyons.

Tom looked the old man over and fairly determined that he had nothing to lose as he had no wife and no daughter and not yet even any prospects for same. If the old man's plan didn't work he was out nothing and if it did work, the old man would likely die of old age before Tom would have any children.

"It's a deal then" said Tom extending his hand. "But you better deliver."

The old Indian shook his hand and said, "Tonight I will call up the earth spirits and they will renew your fields and what you plant will grow very well and when the time is ready I will come back for your first born daughter."

Tom laughed but agreed and went and had himself a drink with the Cutter boys and soon drank himself to oblivion and any recollection of any deal he had made with anyone. He stumbled back to his place well after midnight and fell upon his cot in a stupor.

Morning came and Tom awoke late. He stepped outside with a pondering of what he had to drink the night before and what he should do with what was left of the day ahead of him. But when he looked to his fields he was amazed to see the completely plowed over. The ground was turned into a fine fresh mix of topsoil and what appeared to be fertilizer and organic filler.

He readily got to work planting a new crop and it sprouted and was ready for harvest in record time. Tom became the talk of the town as the most successful farmer in the county. Folk came from miles around and marveled at how well his fields grew right beside others that suffered. Tom acted like he was responsible and knew watering tricks and such and usually only appeared the fool to those that knew better. Some folk thought him a bizarre charlatan and others respected that he could accomplish what they could not, either way Tom was something of a wonder.

That next spring he began courting a Monson girl from Overton and they were married by summertime and by winter she was with child. Tom was overjoyed in his successes and readily forgot everything from the year before.

But when it was time for the child to be born, he did get a little nervous. The field hadn't been producing quite as well as he thought it should and he was reminded of the bizarre old man and his wicked pact. He was however overjoyed when his child was born a son.

Still he resented the pact and the old man but still wished to reap the benefits of same, so he spent some time searching for the old Indian again and was puzzled when none of the Paiutes had any idea of whom it was Tom had spoken with.

Tom had just about guessed that it had all been a dream from a drunken stupor when very late the week after the babe was born, the old man came knocking at his door under a waxing moon.

"What of our bargain?" asked the old man. "Are you not satisfied?"

"I'll tell you true, I was satisfied last season but it seems that as of late, the crops have not done nearly so well as the year before and I am quite concerned over your end of the pact," said Tom. "It seems your work does lack something as time goes on and I sure hope you aren't welching out on me!"

The old man scratched at his chin saying, "These things take some time and I can again employ the earth spirits, if you like, but must ask that when I call again it be two daughters you swear to give me someday."

WHISPERS OUT OF THE DUST — DAVID J. WEST

Tom weighed in his mind the chances of this feeble old man living another winter and the chances on his having a daughter or two anytime soon and he bet. He bet it all.

"Do it, give me the best fields in the county, No! In the territory!"

The old man clapped his hands and this time, this time Tom watched as the dirt rippled under foot and some *things* tore through the ground in a terrible roaring and rushing of turmoil.

"What is that!?" shrieked Tom, wholly amazed at what rending of the ground was happening before him.

"You don't want to see," said the old man.

"Yes I do."

"All right then." The old man clapped his hands again and the surface moved from indistinct swirling through the fields to three waves in the dirt like three wakes of three great invisible ships toward Tom and the old man.

Tom threw up his arms in useless fear and supplication as the old man called in a horrific language commanding the things to rise and rise they did like Leviathans of the deep.

The old man called to the titanic monsters again and they wavered a moment letting Tom get a full look at them up close and personal. Great green worms they were with bodies as big around as a horse. Tom could not fathom how long they were in total but what was exposed above ground was more than wagon team long.

"Judas Priest! Those are big!" exclaimed Tom.

"Now that you see my power will you not reconsider our bargain and cease your prattling of terms? Accept that I will keep up my side as you must keep up yours."

"Well, I assure you that I will have more children though I cannot promise they will be daughters."

125

"I assure you," said the old man. "That you will have many daughters."

"All right then, then I have no problem making a new binding pact with you."

"Good," said the old man, rubbing his hands gleefully.

Tom nodded as he scanned the monsters. "Is there anything the worms can't do? Is there anywhere they cannot go? Do they obey you to the Tee?"

The old man, who no longer seemed feeble or particularly old or even an Indian any longer, nodded saying, "They obey my every command, they cannot die and they cannot get lost and they cannot forgive any trespass against me."

"Perhaps, we can go one step farther with our agreement," said Tom. "One more daughter, and I get to command the worms for one night."

The old man laughed. "Need I remind you, that you cannot command them to devour me, that they shan't ever do nor can they do anything to harm themselves. They will obey every command to the letter and you cannot use them against me. But ask, ask away and I assure you that when the time comes, I will have your three daughters and then I shall have *three more worms*."

"Oh I agree all right," said Tom.

"What will you do? Make your neighbors fields barren? Increase your own crop by having the worms renew the desert? All these things are possible but I will have your children."

"I am deciding, hold on a moment."

The old man held out his hand that looked much more crimson than before and was it possible that the slightest amount of horns were sprouting from his head? Tom wondered, did a spade shaped tail just whip back and forth beneath the old man's coat tails?

No matter.

Tom weighed his choices and said, "Very well, I accept, let us shake and you give me command of the worms for one night." Only too swiftly the old man's hand was in Tom's grasp and the bargain was sealed.

"Now give your command then Thomas Dabney and they will fulfill your demand and I will have thy children soon as they completed thy bidding."

"Worms!" Tom called, and the great green worms did hearken to him. "Get lost!"

The worms wavered a moment, then dove back into the earth and disappeared.

They were never heard from again.

Thwarted, the old man, you know who he was, screamed aloud with a great wailing and gnashing of teeth and he too disappeared in a cloud of brimstone and ash.

And Tom Dabney, he had many daughters many years later and never lost a single one of them.

"An idea, like a ghost, must be spoken to a little before it will explain itself."
— Charles Dickens

Devil Takes the Hindmost

Statement of R. Whortleberry: February 15th, 1896

Now some might have said Jeremiah Mertz had always been a fool, but far be it from me to be so unkind. He wasn't exactly slow-witted, mind you, but he was quite self-absorbed and never did have a lick of common sense in the way that most folk do. He would readily let both his temper and tongue slip through his teeth and speak when he should have been silent and kept his damn ears open—and that has always rubbed people the wrong way. On top of all of that though, I can't say I ever thought him a liar neither, so when he told us how he lost my horse I have to admit to being surprised yet willing to let him pay it back in due time.

This was not a story he had the imagination to make up on his own. After all, Julie had hand stitched his fine tweed coat[47] and there's no way he would have just let anything happen to that if he could have helped it. Besides that his young love Julie made it, he was also a great lover of fine clothing. He always tried to dress his best whenever possible.

---

[47] It has been recorded that Jeremiah Mertz typically spent most of his cowboy wages on his tweed jacket and fancy boots for such dances that typically happened about every three months.

That fine piece of cloth was shredded to ribbons and Jeremiah was certainly lucky to be alive after his encounter.

Here it is as he told me, I just regret that I could not have kept him from being so cock-sure and I further wish I could have averted what happened afterward.

Jeremiah Mertz's Account as told to R. Whortleberry

I borrowed Mr. Whortleberry's horse, Goliath, to ride from St. Thomas on up to Overton for the St. Valentines dance. I was looking mighty forward to my time with the lovely Julie Frost.

We had a grand time. We shared the punch and enjoyed the music. At one time Brian Cook did try to cut in and I wouldn't have it. Julie on the other hand said to allow him one dance with her and leave it at that just to keep things civil. I have always known that Brian wanted her and was incredibly jealous of me. Some people said that he had even paid a visit to the Witch of Rioville[48] in an attempt to make Julie fall in love with him but I never believed any of that rot until last night. He did try to slip Julie some kind of drink from a small vial about a month ago, probably a witches love potion, but she saw him do it and had her father ask him to leave their premises. He swore he would get revenge, but has done nothing more for the last month.

I was allowed by Julie's father to give her a ride home and speak with her afterward upon their porch swing. Time rolls on as we spoke and before I knew it, t'was well past midnight. I said my goodbyes and started for home.

---

[48] Maria Delos Santos, was a local character known for herbs and midwifery for a time. Her age was unknown but she was supposedly very old. Rumor said she was related to the three witches of San Rafael.

It was late and I was sore tired and decided to cut through the swamp by the Muddy [River] to save a little time. In hindsight t'was foolish but I was sore tired. Yes, I had been drinking, but not too much.

I heard a baby's squalling and my first thought was that it was a painter [panther]. But it continued on in a solid cry and I soon found it was a small human baby in the swamp. This was indeed strange but I could not leave a baby alone at night in the swamp. I picked the child up and proceeded to try and put it on the saddle with me but Goliath's [the horse] eyes flared wide, he snorted and panicked and it was all I could do to keep control of the skittish animal. I must say he has never behaved like that afore. I finally mounted him and carried the babe in the saddle in from of me as Goliath acted as crazy as a loon.

We hadn't gone through the swamp for more than a quarter mile when the babe looked up at me and spoke with a deep voice, a saying, 'I don't ride in front. Let me behind you.'

This was the queerest thing I had ever heard in my life but I'm telling you I was compelled to oblige the dark childe. I was still fighting Goliath for control on account of he wanted none of this.

The babe held onto my waist jes fine with its wee hands and we kept heading back to St. Thomas.

Not much farther on Goliath was getting even harder to control, just a panicking and snorting and I was crying and cursing him out loud for his behavior. I felt the babes hands a holding me tight to hang on and then I even felt as if he was scrunching down in the saddle as if holding even a tighter and tighter.

Goliath was side stepping as if to try and watch us like he was afeared of being attacked.

WHISPERS OUT OF THE DUST — DAVID J. WEST

I smelt a horrid stink and was made nauseous in my guts. I wondered at the babes underclothes but then I realized it was the heavy breathing right beside my ears that smelt so terrible.

The babes wee hands seemed to reach farther than they did afore and when I looked down at 'em, I saw not a babes' wee hands but giant hairy paws and claws!

I looked behind me and there was the most ghastly of faces I have ever seen. It was wild and hairy with sharp teeth and yellow eyes! Its big clawed hands started a tearing at me and a ripping my coat up as I struggled to get away.

The demon's roar I shall never, t'was awful as the devil's own choir of imps and demons.

Goliath screamed as the great paws of the monster tore into his neck in an attempt to get and rend me. I lost all control of the animal and we busted a hump farther into the swamp near the river, all the while a fighting and a tearing atop Goliath.

We plunged into the river and the monster still cried for my blood and came after me waving its damned nails like knives.

Waist deep in the river I backed away, trying to escape its clutches. Goliath stamped and screamed and as the demon clawed him again he went under the surface, never to rise again. Then the monster came at me again crying like an ass being eaten by a wolf. I rolled away in the murk and the demon tore after me.

I finally managed to pull my gun and shot the thing straight in the right eye. It cried out and dove deep into the water. Then it was gone and so was Goliath. I crawled to the shore and waited breathless with my gun aimed at the dark water waiting for the thing to rise, but it never did.

WHISPERS OUT OF THE DUST — DAVID J. WEST

I came straight away back to Mr. Whortleberry's and told him everything. He seen my shredded coat and he knows I don't tell no lies ever.

I am done sure that the Witch of Rioville did this thing by a turning Brian Cook into such a beast to get me outta the way so he could have Julie Frost. He already tried to give Julie that love potion and I'm sure he paid the Witch to do this werewolfery to get to me. Everyone knows I could lick him in a fair fight. I will find him, make him pay and all the mystery is solved. Justice will be done.

Report of Randall DeWitt, Clark County Deputy: Feb 16th 1896

Upon investigation of the gunfight in Overton and killing of both one Brian Cook and one Jeremiah Mertz; we found that the two men had shot each other to death and that each of their wounds were fresh at the time of death and that all wounds were within the chest cavity. There were no head wounds as concerned citizen R. Whortleberry asked us to investigate. Case closed.

Obituaries: Rioville Gazette: February 29th, 1896

Maria Delos Santos, age ???, better known as the Witch of Rioville; was found murdered in her home yesterday. Decompositional experts from the Clark County police departments indicated that she had been deceased for at least a week. The killer is still at large. There are no suspects. She was shot dead through the right eye.

"I believe ghost story writing is a dying art."
— H.R. Wakefield

<u>The Groaning Desk</u>

Recollected by B. T. Cutter: December, 1909

"It was right near around New Years, no, it must have been right before Christmas when a fancy city feller came into St. Thomas. Said his name was Wilbur Van Horn[49], or some high fallooting thing like that, I cannot recall exactly now that it has been a few years.

He came to St. Thomas to write about it, he wanted to hear all the old Wild West stories and write them down for some expensive newspaper back east, or maybe it was out west San Francisco or some such. We all had a laugh saying that St. Thomas was not that kind of place so much anymore and that most of those stories were made up or lies or lost and that he shouldn't waste his time in our humble little town.

But then Ma reminded me of how broke we were and we thought more on it and decided that we may as well tell him a lot of stories, embellish them some and see if we couldn't get some money out of him and later maybe some tourism going here. Lord knows we could use the money, am I right?

So we explained we had the only spare room in town and put him up. We also made a tidy sum on some overpriced

---

[49] I could find no record of a Wilbur Van Horn but there was a Willis Van Horn who travelled west from New York around that time.

meals and drinks for him, Lord did he love to eat and drink. Did I mention he was fat? Lord, he was fat as a tick and could eat a hogshead by himself. But his money was good and he was happy and so we were happy. Until he started hearing too many contradictory stories from the kids and he got mad at us and said he thought we had been pulling a fast one on him and he threatened to leave town in a hurry.

We apologized and said that we were sorry, that we were just afeared of telling him the real god's honest truth about our wicked little town. That its gruesome history was quite the embarrassment and we were worried it would ruin any chance of anyone else ever coming here again.

He liked that and promised that on the contrary he would make sure lots more folks came to see our little den of iniquity.

So, we proceeded with caution on what stories we would tell him, but he was beginning to get suspicious and requested that we only tell him tales at his room and one at a time. He said he wanted 'verifiables' and also that he needed a desk, but we didn't have hardly any desks in town for him and we sure didn't want him going to anybody elses house or even one of the other towns and losing our meal ticker. So we told him we would make him a desk.

I didn't have much good wood, wood being scarce in these parts and mesquite sure wouldn't work but then I's remembered that old Hatchfield place and its barn that was just waiting to be torn down. No one had lived there in quite some time not since the days of Black Jack[50]. I seemed to

---

[50] Black Jack Reed passed away on June 27th of 1876 in St. Thomas proper.

recall something happening there when I was a young un but couldn't recollect exactly.

We didn't want the McCormick's complaining that we was taking wood from their property, since the Hatchfield's was theirs now, so we snuck over in the evening just after dark. The barn was a creaking and a groaning and ready to fall down so we just gave it a shove and down she come. I took the foremost rafter from the front and spent all the next day having it scraped and sanded a bit. We then fashioned some legs and a makeshift drawer from a broken dresser for Mr. Van Horn.

I thought once I was done that it looked mighty purty and ma was a bit upset that I had never worked so hard on anything like that for her afore.

Now, Mr. Van Horn had us move the desk into his room and he set it up all fancy like and he seemed awful happy with it. From then on he worked like a dog in his room a typing and taking notes once he had heard our tales of the old days before the railroad and such.

I didn't bother to tell him that we still didn't have a railroad[5] but nodded approvingly when he talked about its great use and importance.

So jest after dark as I'm thinking that life is good and the world is my ointment, Mr. Van Horn storms downstairs and complains that we are a making too much damn noise and that he can't think to write on account of us making the floors creak.

I have no idea what is talking about as most of us had gone to sleep and the rest were quietly talking about the next

---

[5] The railroad spur didn't come to St. Thomas for another three years in 1912.

day's stories to tell him where we knew he would not hear us.

I begged his pardon and told him we would be quieter though I thought he was crazy as a road lizard. No sooner was he right back a hollering and carrying on that tweren't funny anymore.

Now I was curious and I went on up to his room to see what was the matter. Sure enough his desk was making the strangest creaking and groaning as if a great weight was gonna pull it apart. We looked high and low and couldn't see what was making the groaning. The only thing on the desk was Mr. Van Horn's typewriter and notebooks and the creaking didn't stop even when we moved everything.

It kept up like that all night and didn't stop til daybreak.

Mr. Van Horn slept in the parlor that night.

We didn't really talk about it much the next day but always comes evening and the desk a started groaning again. It was a long slow creak back and forth, back and forth, all night long like a pendulum clock it was.

Mr. Van Horn was mighty displeased and I think he thought we might be funning him except he could not figure out how we could pull such a trick.

I sure didn't want to lose my golden noose so I asked the Mormon Bishop to come and bless the house and desk but he toll me he didn't do that for folks that were as disfellowshipped as me. I asked Father O'Leary in Overton to come and bless the house and desk but he said I weren't a good Catholic neither. So I even sent word for Old Chief John, the Paiute medicine man to come and give his Indian blessing on the desk, but he didn't come right away neither.

I was feeling out of luck and knew for sure that Mr. Van Horn would leave us when I wondered about the old

Hatchfield place and knew I should'a done remembered why it was abandoned all these years.

Old Chief John, he come up the next day and he laughed when we told him about the desk and he reminded me of the story.

Way back when, the Hatchfield place was used by some of the outlaws like Black Jack Reed for a hideout as it were. Seems sometime though ole Harry Hatchfield finally had a falling out with the bandits and they argued over how much loot he was to be paid for feeding them and holing them up in his new barn. Rumor had it that he even went so far as to throw down on Black Jack and draw his guns. Now Black Jack was mean as a sidewinder and didn't take too kindly to being threatened by near anyone and he said something to the affect that if Harry Hatchfield cared about his barn so much he could stay there forever. Black Jack he hung Hatchfield right there on the central rafter and I doen't know it but that was the very same rafter beam I used for Van Horn's desk.

The groaning desk had been a gallows pole and the ghost of Harry Hatchfield was cursed to be aswinging on it all night, every night soon as the sun went down. Just as he had that very first night Black Jack hung his sorry ass.

Well Mr. Van Horn got right sick at that development and wrote about it in the daytime at our very kitchen table. He up and left the very next day and we never did hear from him again.

I thought we ought to try and make a little money on the cursed desk but Ma would have none of it. She said that she couldn't cotton to a haunted desk in her own house and it was either her or the bewitched furniture.

No one tells Mr. B. T. Cutter what to do, but she is a very good cook, so I decided that it would be best to get rid of the desk. We took it out and burned it, making it the biggest bonfire for New Year's ever. I reckon old Hatchfield's ghost finally found some peace I suppose from swinging on that spectral gallows pole for the last thirty five years."

"All the dead men will come to life again."
— Wovoka 1890

The Blessing Way

From the memoir of Sara Duke relating to her parents May 1915

Not a lot of things could spook Levi Duke, but fixing up his new bride Eliza's inherited old house did. The house had belonged to Eliza's Aunt Millie, and sat on its own ten acres of nearly treeless property. A lone palm stood tall outside the upstairs bedroom window while a few short fig trees were beside the barn. The house itself had four or five rooms and was all by itself on the outskirts of town. This appealed to Levi, but housework and honey-do's were not his idea of marriage bliss. He agreed to look at the place if only to placate Eliza and suggest later they just sell the place and find a home in Las Vegas. But he didn't think Aunt Millie's place could go for much money, especially in this county and he didn't want to look a gift horse in the mouth either.

They pulled up to the house in Levi's beat up old Whiting Runabout and parked. There was no lawn or driveway to speak of, just a dry laid walkway of stone extending ten feet from the front door. Aunt Millie had kept to herself and only the weed-filled garden outback had ever been given much attention.

"The barn looks like it's about to fall over," said Levi.

"It's fine," said Eliza, "I'm sure you can fix it. This is going to be simply marvelous!"

WHISPERS OUT OF THE DUST — DAVID J. WEST

Levi scowled behind her back as they creaked up the porch and Eliza fiddled in her purse for a key. The storm door almost came off its hinges.

"It always does that, you can fix it," she said.

He responded with a sarcastic grin.

A Model-T pulled up in the driveway and a man in a white tweed suit and straw hat got out. He was rather portly and had even thicker glasses and beady eyes framed above a pencil thin mustache. "You must be Millie Henderson's daughter?" He said in a rather rude tone.

"Actually I'm her niece. And you are?" asked Eliza while simultaneously having Levi stand down.

"I'm John Bryan Farragut, I own the ranch to the south and I am here to state my intentions of asking for, no I'm demanding peace and quiet. Too long your family has seen fit to torment me and mine. The hens won't lay and the cows rarely give milk and it's all because of you and your aunts wretched drumming!"

"I, Mr. Farragut have only just arrived for the first time in over decade. But still I'm quite sure that you must be mistaken, my dear old Aunt Millie would never beat a drum all night. I suggest you complain to your other neighbors."

"There are no other neighbors, I'm very aware of your aunt's queer behavior and soon enough there will be a reckoning!" He then got back into his Model T and drove away in a screech.

"What a bizarre character," said Eliza

"More like rude bastard!" spat Levi.

"Please, we mustn't get off on the wrong foot with the neighbors."

"I think Aunt Millie already did that for us."

"Of course she didn't, that Mr. Farragut is absolutely mistaken. Come on let's go inside and forget him."

Cracking open the front door brought phantom swirls of dust racing into the entry. Shadow and light fought each other for every inch even during midday and it seemed the shadows were winning the battle. Levi wandered through the kitchen and parlor. Eliza threw back curtains and ignored the shifting sunbeams.

"This will be oh so cozy!"

Aunt Millie had decorated her home with two things. Black and white dairy cows of every possible artistic representation and a museums worth of Native American art and artifacts. Indian blankets hung on the wall beside cow curtains and beadwork moccasins dwarfed ceramic cows on book shelves.

"This stuff has got to go," said Levi, groaning. "Aunt Millie had terrible taste."

"I can't throw it away, but we can move it," said Eliza. "Or sell it," she responded, looking at Levi's frown. "Let's go look upstairs."

"I don't think this will work out. We would be much better off in Las Vegas, Darling."

Eliza ignored his protest.

A narrow steep stairway brought them up to a surprisingly large bedroom with a big old bed and a variety of dressers and even more book shelves each straining from their weight of collectibles, candles and oil lamps. More artifacts hung upon the walls including a shallow Indian skin drum and several beadwork shirts. Kachina dolls about a foot tall, stood guard over a dresser along with a few lumps of turquoise and silver jewelry. The Native American theme was quickly wearing itself out with Levi who had been raised back east.

"We shan't want for reading lights," he said, motioning t the multitude of candles and lamps. "There must be hundreds."

"I seem to recall hearing that Aunt Millie only ever slept with the lights on."

"Big old lady like her was afraid of the dark? Ha!"

"Don't make fun, she was very kind and never did find a good man like you."

"I'm just amused is all," he said, before checking the oil in the nearest lamp. "It is queer."

Eliza took Levi's hands, "I can see you don't want to do this, but tell you what, I change the sheets and we spend the night. Sleep on it, and you'll see this can be an amazing place for us. You're gonna love it as much as I did when I was a little girl. And it will be *ours*." She really emphasized the '*ours*'. She always emphasized the 'ours' as far as Levi was concerned, at least with anything that was his, but he paused and thought, her side of the family was putting up this whole piece of property and house. It more than made up for her turning his day shirts into her night shirts.

She could always bring a smile to his face and even while trying to hide it, he broke into a wide grin. "Ok, let's spend the night, then decide what we will do."

Eliza smiled and immediately remade the bed then went downstairs and began dinner. Levi looked about the house a bit more getting to know all of its nooks and cranny's. There were even more cows and Indian artworks along with an incredible amount of stored candles and oil cans for the lamps. He then went outside to take in the view and such. The house commanded a good view of the valley, the river and the town of St. Thomas proper. It was desolate and alone and so different from where he grew up. But there was a mystic appeal, perhaps he could make the best of it at least for one night.

After supper, they talked and read. Then later they exchanged ideas on what they had read. She read from the scriptures as per usual and he was engrossed in a novel about the Civil War.

When darkness came they prepared to retire for the night and Levi lit a single oil lamp for them to use going upstairs, while joking that he didn't know which lamp to choose from. They climbed into the cool bed and said their sweet nothings to each other before falling asleep.

Sometime just after the moon disappeared behind the clouds, but not long after Levi had drifted off, he awoke to hear a scratching at the window. Guessing it was simply the wind and palm tree brushing against the glass he rolled over.

Then his eyes flew open upon the realization that he was quite sure that the palm tree was far enough away from the window that what he heard would have been quite impossible. All manner of wonder and fear at what could be scratching the window at this time of night fell to upon his weary shoulders. What kind of monstrous animal could possibly reach up the twenty foot span?

Nothing.

Well, it had to be an animal of some kind, no man could reach without a ladder. What if it was a man with a ladder? No, it would be easier for a burglar to break in the front door or ground floor windows than the upstairs window. Dear Lord! Was the downstairs already full of robbers? Were they about to be murdered in their beds?

The fear borne of night was rapidly giving way to madness when he became aware now of another sound besides the scratching at the window. He heard it faintly at first, barely piercing the light snoring of Eliza and the ominous scratching at the window, the low yet soft throb of a drum beat.

The primeval beat was steady and in his mind's eye it was the worst most awful sound in the world, a horrible chant of bygone days when savage red men ate raw white flesh.

He somehow found the fortitude to ignite the lamp and face his fears head on, at least with some courage from the light.

And there was nothing there.

No robbers, no red men, no scratching at the window and certainly no skin drum beating to the tune of hell.

Eliza awoke and asked, "Whatever is the matter?"

"Nothing. I just thought I heard something."

"I heard it too."

"What?"

"The drum."

Now whatever daring he had gained in the illumination and lack of fearsome foes was immediately swept back with the revelation of his young bride hearing the drum as well.

He glanced out the window and though he could see that the wind blew on the salty grass under the moonlight, there was nothing he could perceive at the window. The palm was frighteningly illuminated a good few paces away.

"It must have been our imaginations running away with us. Nothing more," he said.

"My imagination hadn't yet time to go anywhere."

"You grew up here. Did you ever hear anything?"

"No," she said, blinking. "I never spent the night though, my parents lived in Overton and I never had to stay after dusk."

He looked at her with worry and confusion. "Perhaps it's simply that I am in an unfamiliar old home that creaks and pops in the night. Yes, that's it."

"Let's go back to sleep, I'm sure it was nothing," she said.

They slowly laid back down and Levi, pulled the blankets up and then gingerly reached out and turned the lamp down until the flame expired.

As the flicker of light vanished the soft throb of the drum came back not a moment after the scratching at the window had also returned.

He leapt out of bed and relit the lamp. He looked again out the window and then under the bed. He opened the bureau and then looked down the darkened stair. Eliza sat upright in bed with a fearful look across puffy eyes.

Levi was frantic now and paced across the bedroom. "No wonder Aunt Millie left you the house. It's haunted!"

"Ridiculous. There must be some other kind of explanation."

"You heard it. You give me an explanation."

She shook her head, "I don't have one."

"We can't both be hearing things after dark, and I must tell you that I was near paralyzed with fright until I heard the drum and had courage enough to light the wick and look about."

"Well I felt it too but hoped it was just a nightmare."

"Oh no, this is real. We both heard the ghost drum. Something terrible is afoot."

Levi experimented several times, extinguishing the lamp and letting a nauseous wave of fear envelope him until the beating of the drum thumped him to his very senses and he would relight the lamp. Time and again he thought he saw great shadowy arms or tentacles covering over the window. They obscured the moonlight though he could still see through them.

Each time with light the horrible darkness, illusions and fear abated as did the ghostly drumming.

WHISPERS OUT OF THE DUST — DAVID J. WEST

They each took to lighting the lamps in the bedroom and looking everywhere throughout the house for where the sounds came from, both the drumming and hideous scratching. They could find the source of neither, and each time the light was snuffed, both the crawling terror and beat returned.

At one point a car's headlights pulled into their driveway and a shotgun was fired twice into the sky and the unmistakable voice of Mr. Farragut shouted that if they didn't cease their infernal drumming, he would kill someone. He then drove away.

It only made the longest night of their lives worse.

As dawn rose red in the east, the aura of despair and dread vanished and so too did the accompanying drumming during the brief moments of blackout.

They poked at their breakfast in silence for some time until finally Levi said, "We shall have to thank your family for offering us the home but there is no way we can remain here. We ought to sell it for any price we can get, no matter how low."

Eliza choked back the tears but nodded.

With the warm sunny blazing overhead, Levi unlocked the door and stepped outside for some air and to think. He was surprised to see a tall old Indian gathering figs from beside the barn. "Excuse me? What are you doing here?"

The old Indian turned and smiled. "Oh, hello. I'm Chief John. You must be Millie's son-in-law?"

"Not that it's any business of yours, but yes I am."

"Ok, good to meet you too then." Chief John then turned around and continued picking figs.

"Just because you used to know Aunt Millie doesn't mean you can help yourself to our figs," said Levi.

"Oh, are you going to live here now?" asked Chief John, without turning around or ceasing picking figs.

Levi was annoyed at the old Indian still picking the figs, not that he wanted them, as well as the old man's casual indifference to his statement. "I am for the moment. Though I believe we shall sell and move back to Las Vegas."

The old Indian grunted at that.

"Say," Levi interjected, "you don't have a drum do you?"

"Not on me," said Chief John, still picking figs. "Do you want one? I gave Millie one years ago. It should still be there." He turned around now and looked at Levi seriously. "She should still have it upstairs in her bedroom, on the wall. To protect her."

"What? How could you know that?"

Eliza was then beside her husband in the doorway. "Please forgive my husband's rudeness Chief John. He isn't familiar with the simple ways out here."

Levi looked to Eliza then the old Indian. "You know each other?"

"Yes, John has been a family friend for years. He did a lot of the yard work and heavy gardening for Aunt Millie."

"Yardwork?" asked Levi, looking at the dry wasteland about him.

Eliza continued. "We spent the night there. Fear and drumming kept us awake all night. We think the place is haunted."

"Oh no, it isn't." said Chief John.

"But the drumming."

"Oh, the drumming wasn't the haunting. The drumming was The Blessing Way. It was protecting you from the spirits outside."

"Spirits?"

"Yeah, they slip through the veil and come around once in a while to try and get in."

"Get in?" asked Eliza.

Chief John smirked and tapped his chest. "Yes, get in—here."

"You mean possession."

"Whatever you call it. But they didn't. The drum protected you," he said, simply. "That's why I gave it to Millie. Lot of bad medicine is drawn to this house."

"That and we are also dealing with threats from a Mr. Farragut, who believes we are doing the drumming to torment him."

"Oh yes, Farragut, he has the spirit of the weasel. He is no good."

"Wait, you just said you gave Aunt Millie the drum?"

"Of course I did."

Levi and Eliza stared at Chief John incredulous.

"I'm sorry for not warning you, I forgot in my old age. A wicked shaman was killed right about where the home was built and the medicine man of the Paiutes at the time planted a sacred palm[52] tree over his grave to keep the evil spirit of the shaman bound to the earth. Unfortunately he misjudged where the body had been buried by the pioneers and the palm was instead planted only somewhere near the shaman and thus could not keep him at rest. So to make up for it, I gave Millie a sacred drum. It is hanging in the bedroom and it keeps the evil spirits at bay. You had to have seen it."

---

[52] The Washington filifera palm tree of the Moapa valley a sacred tree to the Moapa Paiutes. In fact, it is the ONLY palm native to the Western United States.

"We did, but we never realized that was where the sound was coming from."

"Of course you wouldn't. It is only beat on a spiritual level, something from the other side of the veil. It's your spiritual ears that hear it, not these," he said, tugging on Levi's ears.

Levi brushed him off.

"And good news, you should sleep well tonight; the wicked shaman's spirit only rises from the grave and tries to attack every full moon."

"How is that good news?" asked Levi.

"You will recognize him." Chief John gestured with his hands clasped and fingers wiggling. "He looks just like a giant tarantula. I suppose that's why he likes climbing and scratching at the upper windows so much."

"Couldn't we just plant a sacred palm on him now?" Eliza asked.

"Now that is a good idea. Why didn't I ever think of that?" he said, rubbing his chin. "But we would have to find the body first. And we don't know exactly where that is."

"How would we do that?"

Chief John shrugged. "Dig?"

"Could you?"

Chief John held out his hands, "Me? Oh no. I'm getting too old for that. Your fine strapping husband here can do it though. Real quick, I'm sure."

Levi flushed at that. Digging for an evil witch-doctors body in his own back yard was not a pleasant thought. But neither was enduring another night like the last. "Perhaps you might at least have an idea on the best places to try first?"

"Oh sure," said Chief John. "It would have to be on the west side of the house, near the palm."

"How deep would he have been buried?"

"Oh, not too deep. Maybe five, six foot."

Levi scowled at that but proceeded to take the shovel in hand and dig in a spot where Chief John nodded.

He dug several holes like that all over the back yard finding nothing in any of them to the depth of about six feet.

"Are you sure we are even close to the right spot?"

"Oh sure, it has to be right about here."

The day was fading to dusk and Levi felt spent from a full day of fruitless digging.

"The moon still looks pretty full to me," said Eliza.

Chief John nodded, "That it does. I wonder if he can escape through the veil on these nights."

"You don't know!?"

"Anything is possible."

Levi was furious with the old man but Eliza held him back, "What if we watch. Could we see where his spirit emerges?"

Chief John smiled. "You are a very brave Lady, Miss Eliza."

"Mrs. Eliza Duke," snapped Levi.

Ignoring him, Chief John continued, "We could watch and see and remember the place and plant a palm upon it in the morning."

"Oh no, we are not spending another night here," said Levi.

"Levi, we have to fix this thing."

"No, let's just sell it and let it be someone else's problem."

"I can tell you right now," said Chief John, "nobody round these parts would buy it. The market is gone, the mine is gone, and all motivation for people to live out here is gone."

"Levi, please?"

He shook his head. "What are we supposed to do out here when a giant tarantula comes out of the ground? You said it tries to climb the house and get in. You want us to wait out here? No thank you."

Chief John rubbed his chin and said, "Get me the drum and I will stand by you and play, to protect you both. We will see where the evil one emerges and make the spot clear in all of our minds and so be able to trap him in the morning. And of course, once we see him, we will run back into the house."

"Won't he chase us? How fast is he?"

"I don't know that. I haven't seen him move in quite some time."

Levi scowled at that but on Eliza's request he would submit and be a part of the mad scheme.

"Good," said Chief John, "we will trap him yet."

To this they agreed and Eliza went and got the drum and Chief John slowly and quietly began to beat it while chanting an ancient song.

And as the sun fully slipped away and hid itself, darkness fell upon their shoulders with its own weighty resolve. The moon was bright and splashed everything outside in a cold grey luminosity.

And something stirred in the earth, something black that seemed to swallow any faint light reaching from their lantern. It was as if a patch of darkness sucked at the moonbeams and ate them, like a whirlpool of doubt and pain.

Eliza and Levi clutched at each other but remained fixed in place, it was impossible to tell just where the gloom was emerging from the ground as the horrid wave spread outward across the yard. It took them each a moment to realize that Chief John was already playing the sacred drum, beating back against the fear.

The great shadowy spider reared up on all of its legs and swayed at them, menacing and vulgar. It appeared far larger than they had previously imagined and they were now transfixed in place by fear and loathing. Chief John's voice was muffled by the waves of nausea the shadow gave off and Levi felt as if he would retch. Eliza held her breath.

A Model T roared into the driveway and Mr. Farragut jumped out with a shotgun in one hand and a whiskey bottle in the other, but he obviously had no intention of drinking. Instead he had a burning rag stuffed in the top. "I've had enough! I'm gonna burn you out!"

Eliza screamed and Levi tried to cover her.

The giant shadow tarantula shifted its focus to Farragut and lunged. The shotgun and burning cocktail each flared while Farragut shrieked in terror.

Then something broke thru, and they could clearly hear Chief John and his drum and then as the shadow spider loomed ever larger it suddenly shattered as the internal core of shadow suddenly burst into flame. What looked like a shriveled old man in the center burned up and dozens of tarantulas exploded from its core.

Eliza screamed and flung them off of her. Levi swatted at them and cursed.

Chief John however stopped playing his drum.

"Are you crazy? Why did you stop?"

"It is over, it is done."

"Just like that?" asked Levi, accusingly.

Chief John nodded. "Yes, he wanted to see if he was greater than I and if he could outlast my power. But I think it was Mr. Farragut's fire that destroyed the dried mummified body left to Toohoo-emmi."

"Toohoo-emmi?"

"That was his name."

"Is it really over?"

"It is."

"But if he plagued Aunt Millie all this time, and all you could do was give her the drum then how? Why now?"

"I wouldn't have thought we could burn him like that."

"Was he really trapped here? Did we even really need a palm over his grave?"

"Maybe once, but I truly didn't know where in the backyard he was buried. Again, it is over and you have your home back and in peace. Another palm might look nice there but you don't need it."

Eliza asked, "How do you know he wanted a body? How did you know we could defeat him tonight? How did you know his name?"

"Because he was my brother. And I have been waiting for the right time. I never knew until today that it was today. I had worried that in my old age I might run out of time and he would be left to inflict his harm on the inhabitants of this land longer than I could be around. But it is done, the mistakes of the past are finally reconciled in a large part thanks to a terrible man."

"I don't understand."

"Everyone has value, even bad examples. Even the murderous Farragut served a purpose for the greater good."

"I don't like this one bit," said Levi. Eliza brushed his cheek and tried to calm him.

"But the home is ours and we are free of that evil?"

Chief John nodded. "It is done. I wouldn't tell anyone that you saw a giant shadow tarantula bite Mr. Farragut though. Better tell folks he came over and had a heart attack. Farewell."

He walked out into the night and they never spoke to him again.

"After the horse dance was over, it seemed that I was above the ground and did not touch it when I walked."
— Black Elk

Chief John Rides Again

Eulogy delivered by Charlie Wisespirit[53] April 6th, 1921 along with some cataloged witness[54] reactions.

"I say the following not for Old John but for the White Man, that they may know a little more about what kind of man John was and that they may know more of his people and this land that he cared for as a steward, and not a land owner. Old John owns just as much now as he did when he was born, but we are wealthy beyond counting for having had his presence in our lives.

This is how I will honor him.

The old ways are dying and none of us can bring them back, they slip through our fingers like the wind. The past is a phantom that we cling to but always comes evening and it disappears like the stars in the dawn, doomed by mornings first light. Yet the dawn too is the future and what it brings tomorrow no man knows.

I cared for my mother's elder brother Old John in the last year of his life. He had grown too weak to ride his horses

---

[53] This was held outside by the "Big Ditch" close to the Paiute dwellings.
[54] Cataloged witnesses include the Gentry's, Perkins, Dukes, Ferguson's, Mayberry's, Judkins, Albrics, Sellers, Nutter, Whortleberry's, Cutters and most of the Moapa Paiute tribe.

or hunt in the hills. He could not tend his garden or make his own meals, but he was a good man, a wise man and a truer friend I have never known. I will especially miss his sense of humor and playful manner. John was also our medicine man for as long as anyone can remember. He was young but he was the shaman of our tribe when the Mormons first came and he has always looked out for his people. We will never forget him.

Always he strived to do what was right and his courage was as great as any mans.

When he was a boy he was kidnapped and sold into slavery by the Shoshone and managed to escape from them. He had been taken far to the southeast but he found his way home through the wide desert. It was there that he became a man and learned to talk to the Great Spirit.

It was only later as he matured that he said he learned to listen too."

[Audience laughed]

"There are many other stories of John I could relate and some of those many of you will already know. What was important is that he loved his people and did all he could to watch over them and help them become a strong people.

As I began, the old ways are dying. The tribal elders expect that I will sacrifice my two horses that Old John may ride up to the next world, but I will not."

[There was gasp from the audience here, and some few protests from older Paiute elders.]

"Old John Two-Hawks loved to laugh, he was original, he was different from most men and I will honor him in a new way, a different way that I truly believe he would enjoy."

[Mr. Wisespirit then left the makeshift pulpit and went through the gathered crowd to where he had parked his old

Model T. The audience with curiosity fully piqued followed. Mr. Wisespirit who had taken up a flaming torch.]

"In the old ways we would take a living thing like a horse and we would kill it and burn it. So that our departed loved one might have a mount in the afterlife. But I will not kill something Old John loved in this life to give him in the next."

[Again several in the crowd jeered or complained at this most unorthodox behavior.]

"Instead, I will burn this Model T and when all the others come riding up on horses in the next world, Old John will drive up in that Model T and be just as well off as any of them!"

[With that Mr. Wisespirit took the torch to the car and it went up in a great blaze of belching black smoke and orange flame.]

"Oh Great Spirit, recognize your son John Two-Hawks and welcome him!"

[The burning car sparked and crackled as fire jetted over it. And it was reported by witnesses that the powerful winds came up suddenly and caused the flames to grow and expand shimmering much greater than any could have possibly expected.

Some witnesses claimed this was just a chaotic dust devil that came serendipitously but I doubt it.

Smoke shifted into the most unusual shape mimicking a great black car and it seemed to swirl about over the top of the heads of the gathered audience in the parking lot. Some witnesses swore they heard a great laughing that sounded just like Old John's before the black dust devil swirled higher and disappeared just as suddenly as it had arrived.]

"I see him now! He is driving the car of smoke and spirit up to the next world! He is happy and he wants you to be happy! His work here is done. Thank you Great Spirit."

✞ ✞ ✞

I can see him now too in my mind's eye, putting pedal to the metal of a ghostly Model T chasing the specters of the deer and antelope, racing his ancestors and feeling the electric light speed with the changing of worlds. This is not a mockery, this is a celebration of vitality and a rebirth of both the new and the old, together again in that eternal cycle of life from one plane to another. There is no end, but sometimes we can pick how we get there.

And Old John is still laughing somewhere on the highway to Heaven behind the wheel of a spectral Model T Runabout.

"All those persons interred within the St. Thomas semitary shall be forthwith removed, exhumed and transported to a new semitary located within Overton, Nevada, that shall be known as the Lake Mead Semitary. There will be no survivors."

— Arthur Wraxell: Rioville Gazette May 1934

Wisp of a Thing

Stanza by Anonymous: December 1934

I saw a wisp of a thing in St. Thomas town
Kingly it was, though it bore no crown
Dark and majestic, both sad and proud
I was taken aback to see that it wore a shroud
For though I work with the living and the dead
It bodes not well to hear what the latter has said
I will rise again and again and again it cried
And in my fear and shock my heart almost died
Do not call up what you cannot put down
For the spirit of this place may drink deep and drown
But the call of its heart will beat on and sound
Until all who walk over will feel this ground
Shake and tumble, explode and roar
Til the dead come and walk once more.

"Of all ghosts, the ghosts of our old loves are the worst."

— Sir Arthur Conan Doyle

There was a Woman Dwelt by a Graveyard

The statement of Donald Wagner: May 25th, 1935

"In the months prior to Lake Mead flooding my old homestead I was given much to driving back and forth between the new and the old place. I was hiring day laborers to help with my move and ranching and such, I'm not as young as I used to be and the ranch needs a lot of work beyond my years and strength.

As you know very well, one of the laborers I picked up was an older feller, name of Thomas Bickersham who grew up around here he says and has been gone since he was a young'un. I do not recall any family by that name in these here parts, but he was a good hard worker. He knew the lay of the land so has definitely spent some time here before, even if that is not his Christian name.

On the first day of Mr. Bickersham's help we were passing by the old graveyard of St. Thomas, all of the graves having been removed to the new in Overton and we both saw a woman standing there in the morning and again at twilight.

It was hard to see her exact features but she had a long grey dress and long dark hair that was flying in the wind quite unkempt and wild, though I don't recall there being any wind that day when we stopped the truck later.

We saw her again the next day both in the early morning light and the gloomy twilight of evening. Mr. Bickersham seemed especially unnerved though I was not sure as to why exactly. He claimed it was for shore not anyone he had ever known nor spoken too. I suspected he may have been a bad liar but he was still a good ranch hand. So I didn't worry.

I seemed to recall a tale told of a woman who dwelt by the graveyard for the last few odd years and I had never paid it no mind. But having seen her for myself now I did wonder at why she was there and what she was doing in that lonely place. Some of my other hands had spoken of seeing her before and to tales relating to this heartbreak or that and even perhaps that she was a lost soul from when the town had seen wilder days. Some others said a ghost but I thought not as her dress did not look as old as that, nor did I believe I have ever seen a ghost either.

She did not look like a spook to me.

And on the third day we again saw the woman in the graveyard. I found it especially strange as I am shore that there are no more graves there, all of them having been moved on to Overton's new Mead Lake Cemetery[54] by the last couple months or so. There is no good reason that the woman should be spending so much time in such a place that the federals claim will be under water in a few more months. When I looked in the rearview mirror I could not see her anymore and I wondered to where she had gone.

---

[54] The Mead Lake Cemetery was eventually renamed the St. Thomas Memorial Cemetery.

Saying as much to Bickersham only made him cringe and he looked nervously out the rear window, admitting that he was afraid of spooks.

But I said I didn't believe in spooks and told Bickersham that I meant to talk to the woman if she was indeed there as we would pass by that evening. Bickersham said that was fine, but as evening came on and our work was nearly done, he made excuse after excuse to not go with me back to the homestead and thereby have to go past the graveyard. I said fine and left him to make out for himself over night at the new ranch.

As I drove closer to the old graveyard I did not see the woman and was quite perplexed as I had fully expected to see her again after so much routine. But I did stop the truck and take a look around to sate my own curiosity on the matter. It was getting dark and I found no sign of any person being there save for the marks where the old graves had been exhumed.

It was then that I realized that the woman I had seen on those previous occasions had not been in the graveyard proper but right outside the boundaries of same. I walked to that place and saw that the ground there was somewhat sunken and denoted the possibility of that being another grave outside of the proper accounting of same and that it had been missed.

I then wondered if she was indeed a spook and I alone was privy to her sorrow and struggle at being left behind and that she was in mourning to having been forgotten and that soon enough her unattended and forgotten grave would be under the waters of Lake Mead forever more. This and the sunset made me wax more poetic than usual and I smiled to myself.

I then drove on home thinking I would inquire with Old Man Perkins about the possibility of a missed grave and whether there was anything more to the woman in the graveyard story dating back to the pioneers.

That night I slept fitful like. I was roused multiple times thinking I had heard screams but when I woke there was no sound but the crickets and even then they weren't too loud. In my mind's eye I thought I saw the woman's face, even though I had ever got a good look at it afore. I also thought I saw Bickersham's leering face and it made me uneasy.

Next morning I was called away on account of a broken fence and rather than drive all the way back out to the south forty to get Bickersham, I went and fixed the fence myself.

When I stopped at Gentry's I saw Old Man Perkins there as I have told you earlier, and I asked about the grey woman.

He said that he had heard about her for some few years but that it was only that—years, like about forty he said, no longer. Folks only started seeing the spook when he was about twenty five he said. Some suspected that it was the spook of Molly Trager but then no one knew why she would haunt anyone.

More likely he said it was the Calico gal from Rioville who had come up on one of the last steamships and plied her trade her for a few months, then one night she just disappeared, most everyone figured she had just used up the town and moved on, but it wasn't long after that, that folks started to see the grey woman at the graveyard.

Funny thing was he told me, that nobody ever saw her with another witness, they were always alone. I explained that both Bickersham and I had both seen her together several morning and evenings in a row and that Bickersham always had quite a fright for it.

His eyes raised at that and he enquired as to who this Bickersham was. I replied that he was my hired help for the summer and that I had my suspicions of him but nothing solid. Old Man Perkins needed something to do beyond play cards with the Garvy boys so he rode along with me.

We stopped at the old cemetery and I showed him the spot where I had seen the grey woman and he agreed that it looked suspect. Being that it was right outside of the graveyard there weren't no law to prevent us from taking a look. I took the shovels from out of the back of my truck and we dug into the rocky ground.

Not even two feet down and we found it. Bones and a grey dress, the very same faded ash grey that I had seen the woman wearing. Strangely, the ring finger on her left hand had a gold wedding band? But Old Man Perkins was near to sure that it was indeed the Calico gal.

We then promptly drove back to tell you [Sheriff Warner] and alert the other county authorities. They come and claimed the remains and only then did I head back toward the ranch house.

It was nigh on dusk when I found myself driving on back to the new ranch. I guessed that the mystery was solved and that now that the Calico gal's body had been found she could be laid to rest proper with the others from the graveyard and not worry over her grave being forgot and left to flood over.

As I pulled into the driveway of my ranch house I noted that no new work had been done on the place. I was upset that Bickersham had taken my absence to mean a day of loafing but I soon found him in the garage.

He was expired. A final note of confession was crumpled in his dead left hand. I pulled it loose and read:

I, Travis Longstreet, whom you knew as Thomas Bickersham do hereby confess my crimes, done committed in my youth of forty years agone. I dids't murder the woman I loved, a lady of ill repute name of Jessica Steinhem as she would not quit her sinning and marry me. Afterward I dids't attempt to do the proper Christian thing of burying her in the graveyard. I did however miscalculate on account of the dark and my drunkenness and I done buried her outside of it. I knew when I saw her spectre that my past would not go away and she should come for me someday as she said she would when I kilt her.

May God have mercy on my soul.

P.S. Please bury me in a different graveyard than her.

Wrapped about Bickersham's neck, in the fashion of a hangman's noose, was a ragged ash grey dress, still dusted with fresh dug soil while a gold wedding ring lay refused on the ground beside him."

"St. Thomas did not die. It was murdered. Not maliciously, but definitely with aforethought. St. Thomas was surrendered, given up, sacrificed, if you will, for the good of the many."
— Jori Provas

Bury Me Deep

Diary of John Kane: June 11ᵗʰ 1938

Because I extended a kindness once to an old man, I became involved in a terrible happening shortly before the waters of Lake Mead did drown my home of St. Thomas.

I saw him broken down beside the road and I stopped like a Good Samaritan to help. Little did I know, I should have turned the other cheek and kept driving on down the road. So I became acquainted with the old man and he did call upon me from time to time and I was perhaps his only friend in the county. He did ask favors sometimes while never granting any himself.

Everyone in those parts agreed that the dying old man was an evil old scut. No one knew where he was from or who he was exactly, just another lost stranger looking to hide away from the world; and in what more out of the way place than in this forgotten shell of a town could a man try and escape his past? I never did get a straight answer from him myself.

Plenty guessed at his former professions and all seemed to agree that whatever it was must have been heinous indeed. Mary Bickford said she saw him standing naked in a ring of fire in the night, beckoning to the dark with arms outstretched and wide, calling to some unseen force on the wind. She did say she thought he had strange tattoos all over his chest. And Steven Walpole once said he saw people he described as Black Viziers holding conference with him upon the autumnal equinox and Doc Knox verified same. Even I saw him another time with what looked like a bat upon his shoulder. He appeared to be talking with it before it flew off into the twilight. The Paiutes avoided him at all costs, saying he was bad medicine.

He had to hire an outside woman[56] from Las Vegas to care for his laundry and meals. Few it were he talked with and even less that got more than two words from him. Some said his name was Samuels and still others claimed it was Rogers, either way he kept much to himself now didn't he?

Sometime in the early winter it was, when—let's call him Sam Rogers then—he fell deathly ill and called for Father Murphy over in Pioche for the Last Rites, but as the devils luck would have it, the Father had been called away to some argumentative commotion involving the tribe over in the Valley of Fire and in no way could the Father arrive in time for the dying man. Next, the call for some type of religious confession fell to Bishop Winters who readily complied with the strange request.

We never found out exactly what Sam Rogers confessed to the poor Bishop, but when the holy man left Rogers's bedside he was quite shaken. Not an hour later, near the stroke of midnight Rogers died with a loud gasp crying out to the handful of witness's, myself included, *I was wrong! They come for it yet! Bury me deep!* before keeling over with his long tongue lolling out. That was the first time I did

---

[56] Meaning from outside of the local populace.

get a look at the weird blue tattoos that were upon his chest. They were strange characters of a sort I could not designate. All arranged in a circle spiraling inward.

Relating to his final words, one knew for sure what *"it"* was, but there was quite a list of possibilities and nearly all involved treasure of one kind or another.

Rumors like cracks in the ice spread and soon enough there was talk that Rogers's treasure must be somewhere on his property. While the man had lived in relative if not humble squalor this did nothing to abate the rumors. The Bishop's soon permanent departure back to Salt Lake only increased the volatile suspicions since there was no longer anyone who could say what the dying man's real concerns had been.

Though Rogers had made a will of his meager estate to one Kate Blanchard, his laundress, she too died within a fortnight leaving no explanation for the wild accusations of both hidden treasure and sorcerous evil. It seemed with every passing day someone added their pittance of knowledge to the legend until the fable was far larger than it ever could have been in truth.

Within a week of Kate's passing, the grounds round Rogers's place were littered with failed treasure digs and torn apart walls. Even his cistern was pumped dry to investigate whether he had something hidden in the well. The place caught fire one night and there was no hint of anything left within the scanty walls or crumbling foundation. Still, folk dug about the place and guessed at what might be vague hints of treasure and gold for surely it must be something of great value. With the reservoir's swift approach, much anxious prospecting was done and still there were no answers.

I have been remiss in explaining the very first place that the treasure seekers did look—Rogers's grave itself. He did after all ask to be buried deep and sure enough, though the county mortician prepared his corpse with a fine black suit, there was no other article on his person when his pine box was lowered into the ground. There was no treasure with him. Certainly no bible verses or priestly element spoke at Samuel Rogers's funeral. Kate recited a poem written by the mad poet Justin Geoffrey. It seemed fitting enough, rather than a Christian sentiment that we all knew Rogers would have mocked.

I was surprised at the simple Latin stanza that Rogers himself had left for his marker stone however.

Vermis Sum Portarium

Of those present there was not a one of us who could not understand it, save Kate, and she did not answer for it after looking upon the stone. She was weeping and I never had the heart to ask her what it meant before she too had passed away so soon thereafter.

Despite his grim directions upon his deathbed, Rogers was only buried the standard six feet deep, the same as any other saint or sinner.

Grave robbers did roughly exhume his casket less than a week after his internment but if they found anything, no one heard more about it. I myself went and reburied what the robbers had left. Soil had been cast about rather haphazardly. Shovels full were sprayed out in every direction as if the grave robbers had been in a terrible hurry to examine the casket.

I spoke with Bill Johnson who said he found Rogers grave interrupted as such nearly a week after I did. He too did rebury the casket post-haste for he did have an awful feeling while there and did not want the body exposed to the night sky. The moon makes men strangers, he said, and who knows what it might do to a corpse as wicked as old man

Rogers? He was taking no chances at letting Rogers possibly walk amongst us again. In spite of my modern outlook, I worried that Johnson had a very strong point indeed.

Not a week later from that episode, just before sunset I was driving down the county road past the cemetery and noticed the coffin sitting propped upright in the grave upon a dirt mound facing the setting sun. I knew for certain whose grave it was. I walked up casually and saw that grave robbers had tampered with Rogers's resting place and this time in what seemed broad daylight. Fresh dirt was showered outward in every direction and I wondered a moment if his coffin hadn't been rejected by the earth itself.

This was pure foolishness, he was but a man and I should not take to flights of fancy on such things. But why would treasure hunters dig him up again, surely everyone in the county had heard that he had been dug up already by now and whatever he could have possibly had relating to the treasure was surely gone.

But as I leaned down to replace the lid and do the proper thing, I was taken aback that there beside his desiccated body was something added to his coffin.

A small black notebook lay upon Rogers's chest. It was open and the wind was sifting through the pages like a ghostly hand reading excitedly.

I thought to close the lid and rebury Rogers and leave the dark notebook where it lay, but my own curiosity got the better of me and I picked it up to see what was written inside.

It was in code with letters, symbols, planets and numbers I recognized but none of it making any sense to my eyes. It was indeed similar to some of the tattoo that was still visible near his collar bone. This was surely the workings of a mad man. The only word I saw in the entire volume that I knew was the single scrawled name of *Marian* on the inside flap.

Who was she? Could she have left this memento for the wicked old sorcerer? There was no one by that name that I knew of anywhere. And if it was a gift for the departed why not close the lid and keep him from the gathering ravens and flies? It was getting dark and I had no further patience or knowledge for such eerie happenings. I reburied his casket but I kept the notebook.

I looked the thing over again by lamplight as shadows danced across the walls. Some message ached to escape from the prison of these pages but I had no way of unlocking that door. I thought on numbered sequences and exchanging the letters but none had an effect that I could perceive. Exasperated at the long night of fruitless wonderings I went to sleep and had fitful dreams.

Somewhere on the edge of the sleep not far from nightmare I caught sight of a dark rider coming over the red splashed desert, what he brought with him I could not tell but it brought shivers to my spine. It seemed like he was blind, as if he could not see me but was indeed hunting. I was somewhere beside the river and bound to stay on one side. I tried to move silently away from this grim figure but as the rider neared me, a black sticky substance like tar flowed out from the feet of his horse's hooves like a stretching shadow. This darkness creeped and rose up sweeping like a dark wall looming over me, ready to crash and bury me beneath its cyclopean weight. I ran but could not move fast enough to evade its crashing crescendo, and then all went dark just as daylight pierced my eyelids.

After three nights of that dream I fully intended the throw the notebook away and be done with the whole of the awful mystery but something stayed my hand and the black book remained upon my table. I cannot say why for its very presence so unnerved me, but I could not bring myself to burn it.

I worked again until sundown and drove back to my place with a sad song upon my lips that I could not name. The name *Marian* repeated itself to me and I wondered again at who she might be to have any involvement with Roger's.

The whole of St. Thomas was now nearly deserted and few enough there were left for me to confide my sleepless questions. I drove past the burnt remains of Rogers's place and then found myself passing Kate Blanchard's place. A car was out front and a young woman was packing. She was a pretty brunette and had a lantern out as she worked. I stopped and asked if she needed any assistance.

"No, I'm fine. I'm Marian Blanchard. I'm just here to get some things that my mother may have left. I understand that what's left of the town will be under water soon."

To say I was flabbergasted was putting it mildly. I explained my interest and the curious occasion of our meeting. She was dubious and I can't say that I didn't blame her had I not been living the mystery myself.

I helped her finish gathering the few meager belongings and we shared a pot of coffee. I soon found out that she had not spoken with her mother in quite some time.

"I suppose she had been so absent in my life that I never really felt her loss. I do hope you understand I'm not trying to be callous. I do love my mother but it's almost like I never knew her. She never had time for me, always chasing the latest dream and wondering about the stars and such. I don't think I mattered to her since she never really got over my father."

"Your father?"

"I never knew him. Compared to him, Mother was the ideal parent. I understand he was quite a world traveler and something of a mystic or even a magician."

"That can be a lot to live up to," I said. Smiling so as not to offend.

"Mother wrote me a letter a couple months ago saying she thought she had found him and that was the last time I heard from her until Mrs. Mayweather informed me that Mother had passed away last week. I had the devil of the time getting here. I was almost afraid the town would be under water before I could arrive."

It took me a few moments to let things fully sink in and then I realized that she had a much prettier face but was incredibly similar in nose and cheek structure to Rogers.

"You never knew your father at all? What he looked like or anything?"

"I never met him but I saw a picture once of him from twenty years ago. Mother must have it here somewhere. She was obsessed with him and I think that's why she lived such a gypsy like life, trying to keep up with him and perhaps catch him again someday."

She rifled through a few dressers and produced a picture, bent, faded and cracked with age but it was Rogers nonetheless.

"That's him all right. We knew him as Samuel Rogers. He was living here," I said. "But he died shortly before your mother under strange circumstances."

"You knew him? He is dead? Why didn't you tell me?"

"Hey, I only just pieced it together. You didn't say you were Sam Rogers's daughter."

"I'm sorry, it's not something I'm proud of. You were present at his death?"

"I was. I knew him, though not well. He did request my presence at his death for whatever reason, Lord only knows. He said some strange things right before his passing. If I told you, do you think you might know what he meant?"

She shook her head. "I can't say I would. You can try."

I liked the way she said that, maybe too much. "He said, that he was wrong, someone was coming for *it*? And to bury him deep. But no one knew what he was wrong about, who that someone might be or what it was. Most of the town assumed *it* was treasure and his place has been looted and dug up several times over. Even his grave has been dug up and robbed three times over though I was there when he was buried and he had nothing on his person."

She took a moment to ponder all I had said, I wondered for a moment if she did know something and was guessing what she could trust me with.

"You say his coffin was dug up three times? Are you sure nothing was taken? How can you be sure?"

"Well I was there when we buried him, he had nothing on him but a cheap suit, no offense. Then someone dug him up again to have a look. I buried him a second time and then a friend did a third time and I did again only three nights ago. His coffin had been fully exhumed."

She looked at me scornful like and I suddenly felt bad, I was after all talking about this young woman's father, I had meant no disrespect.

"You really never found anything? Are you sure no one took anything?"

"Well, now that you mention it," I said, scratching my chin, "I did find something odd that someone left there."

"Left there? Where? What was it?" She was urgent now and I was taken aback at her complete change of character.

"It was a small black notebook, it had writing in it but it's all in code, a curious gobbledygook that I couldn't make heads or tails of. Only one word in it could I understand."

She looked at me sharply like a cat about to eat a rat. "Well? What did it say?"

"Marian, it just had your name. Marian."

"Why didn't you tell me this sooner?"

"I didn't know you yet, I didn't want to offend you or anything and I only just figured out that Sam Rogers was your old man anyway."

"Old man," she laughed. "Yes, I suppose he was."

Her laugh did not sound like a healthy jest and I was now the uncomfortable one, but again I had no idea of all the things she and her mother had been put through by the crusty old wizard so who was I to judge?

"I need to see the notebook right away, and I want to look at my *old man's* property, there very well could be some things the rest of you may have missed."

"I never dug around his place, it wasn't my way to pry after such things. It burned down, I don't know that there is much left."

"Some things lost on the borders of dusk were never meant to be found," she said. "But I mean to find and shine them to the light before shutting the door."

I nodded though I didn't get her meaning. She got in my truck. We left her car behind and the lamp burning because I thought we would soon be back I was very wrong.

"I want to see his grave too. You understand don't you?" she asked, in a sweet yet sad way.

"Of course." It couldn't hurt anything to let her have her goodbyes, could it?

We drove to my place to get the notebook as it was the closest of all our destinations and upon stopping there I ran inside and got it. She eagerly perused the thing as if she could readily understand the madness. "You know what it says? I asked.

"A little. It is based on a code my mother and I used when I was very young."

"So why did I find it laying on his chest in the graveyard? No offense," I added, as we bumped along the back country dirt roads on our way to the cemetery.

"I suspect perhaps it was with him all along. In his breast coat pocket perhaps and this last time that he was disturbed it fell out of his pocket and onto his chest."

"Why would anyone do that?"

"I don't think anyone did. I think it was his dark energies reacting and playing with his tomb."

"Yeah, but why did Rogers have it?"

"I believe he is the one who taught the code to my mother in the first place. It is something members of his Order would use."

"Order? What Order?"

"The Brotherhood of Hermes Trismegistus, of course! Granted, I was told that he was thrown out for conduct unbecoming and in response he made a vengeful threat to open the doors between worlds."

I said nothing, steering the truck around the winding roads in the dark.

"There is something that must be done and I need your help. You won't like it."

I certainly didn't know what the hell she was talking about. "What do you need me to do? I am expensive." I teased.

"My father was a very dark magician hoping to open a doorway. His own death was to be the key to open it upon the full moon. We have only a very short time to prevent this."

"I'm just a cowhand who happened to help out an old man once. I do not understand a lick of what you just said back there."

She was pouting now and if I live to be a hundred I don't believe I'll ever understand women, let alone one who talks magic at me as if I'm supposed to be in on the great cosmic joke.

She looked at me disbelieving saying, "Stop teasing. You probably know all about this from my father already. You must know I am his Moon Child and was bound to be here and discover these things. My mother always told me someday I would understand, and now, now I do. Upon his death exactly twenty eight days later I must fulfil the covenant and hold back and lock the gates one more time."

"Uh huh. Now what exactly do you want me to do, besides take you out to see your old man's final resting place?"

"Oh, it cannot be his final resting place. He told you specifically he must be buried deep and I know just what he had in mind when he came to this wretched town."

"Hey! I like it here! It's a damn shame what's gonna happen to St. Thomas!"

She looked at me again and seemed to have resigned herself that I was no magician to understand what she talked about.

We pulled up to the graveyard and there once again was Rogers coffin, sitting upright forced out of the ground.

"Impossible," I said, staring at the thing illuminated by the headlamps.

Marian looked at me like she couldn't make up her mind. Worrying that I was playing her when I didn't even understand the rules of the game. "His headstone so fitting."

"What does it mean?"

"It says 'I am the Worms Gatekeeper'. It's a cruel joke considering what he meant to do. Get him in the back of the truck, we need to rebury him deep."

"And where is that?"

"Somewhere the water is swiftly rising, somewhere he can be buried deep."

I picked up Rogers casket and slid it into the back of the truck. It was lighter than I remembered at his funeral by a good few stones. "And now?"

"Drive us south, toward the Salt Mine, let me see the rising waters."

We drove down the old county road toward the Salt Mine and where the Virgin River met the Muddy.

Marian was quiet now and I could in no way discern her thoughts. She watched the sky which was rapidly turning a deeper shade of blue as the pale glow in the west was fading fast.

"There!" she said, pointing at some outcropping of rock. I did note that we were perilously near the rising waters of the reservoir.

"That water is rising awful fast. Hugh Lord almost lost his car just a couple days ago while fishing this close. And you want me to bury him deep? I don't know that I have it in me to go much deeper than six feet."

"That's not what he ever meant by bury him deep. The waters will be his tomb and his prison, holding him fast far below the surface."

"If that's what you say you want for your old man, that's' fine. But we could drive farther down and just throw him in with chains wrapped around him to sink if that's what you are looking for." I was surprised at this sudden bout of being an accomplice to this insane venture. What was I thinking?

She just gave me that look again, the kind that would melt you on a winters day and shook her head. "It has to be here and now, you must know this."

"No! I don't know any of this. It's all crazy and I'm being caught up in it like a fool."

She stopped pacing out the spot I should dig and said, "You put on a convincing show. I almost believe that you don't know what we are doing here, but I'm growing weary of the game. I won't fall for it to just have you laugh that you caught me. Do your job. Dig the hole and together we shall bind the darkness."

I put the shovel to the earth where she had designated, grumbling about binding the darkness. This was truly the strangest night of my life.

The soft soil made digging easy but as I was down about six feet, the mud began to collect and I suspected the pit would soon be full of water. "We better do whatever you're planning awful quick!"

"Put him in the hole," she ordered, as she continued mumbling, while reading something from the dark notes.

I pulled out the casket and let it down into the grave. I had miscalculated and it was too short.

"Your games do not amuse me," Marian said.

Quickly I took the spade to the edge and started giving it another foot to fit.

I wiped away the dirt and sweat and just looked at her. This game of magic was nearly more than I could bear. I truly was in over my head here.

I dug away just enough for his casket to fit. My feet were now completely mired in mud as the ground at the bottom was soaking up the rising waters first. I put the casket in with an unceremonious drop and then Marian helped kick dirt over this soon to be unknown grave of her father.

I shoveled in spade after spade full all the while watching the lake waters inch closer to us. By the time I finished, the waters were pouring into the last few inches of the plot.

Then there was a rumble, and dark waters flushed back as something rose to the surface. Marian screamed and I was in shock as the coffin surged from the mud and filth.

I saw no animated movement from the body itself but somehow the hand and arm had reached out of slime at the coffins ascension from the earth. They were smeared with wet earth and it was a truly horrible sight. The lid had partially snapped off and I saw the old mans wretched face leering in a deaths head grin. His shirt and coat were pulled back and that bizarre spiral tattoo faced the open night sky.

But then it stopped and just lay there upon the surface as water splashed about the edges.

"We have to do it again and find a way to keep him bound until the waters have him contained."

"And how would I do that?"

She shook her head and wiped away tears with her shawl. "There! Let's drive up there and dig a fresh grave, we should have at least another hour or two."

To this insanity I reluctantly agreed. I picked up the now waterlogged and muddy coffin, attached the lid again and putting it in the truck, drove just up the valley a short distance and proceeded to dig yet again. This time, when I took a breather, Marian dug too. It was a welcome change of pace.

"Is this what you wanted?" I asked, breathing heavy.

"This is beyond anything I want. This is a necessity."

We had him in the ground and once again the bottom had turned to mud. I shoveled the soft ground and rock over him. This time, I threw in a few large stones as well. Anything to make it all the more difficult to return.

As I finished the waters were again washing over the freshly dug ground and it seemed that there was a movement beneath the murk.

I looked to Marian and she answered the horror by saying, "Park your truck upon it and I will repay you."

It was mad but I agreed and drove the truck over the grave as the waters were splashing over the running boards. I jumped out and ran to the shore as the truck rumbled as something was pushing from beneath with great force.

"Yes. He is contained here and soon the purifying water will hold him deep. It is done."

I looked at her and decided I had had enough of this madness and would never ever again extend help to an old man broken down beside the road or to a young grieving woman clearing out her mother's place.

As I looked to starry night, between the nearly full moon and Venus, I could swear I saw an especially dark starless spot swirling like a shadowy whirlpool directly above. As we sat there and watched the waters lapping over the top of the truck that dark spot in the sky gradually faded away.

We stayed until morning, every few hours moving back from the newly found shore, keeping an eye on that grim place in the lake.

I cannot explain any this bizarre happening and that is why I have written it down, so someone might someday hear of it and understand.

There are dark things in the world, dark happenings that no one else sees, but they abide there on the borders of nightmare, waiting.

"It is an ill thing to meet a man you thought dead in the woodlands at dusk."
— Robert E. Howard

Return of the Toad

Journal of David J. West: September 21st 2015

If there is one thing I know when I look out across this vast American west, it is that we inhabit a haunted land. Where we live has been dwelt upon since time immemorial and I do not mean just the last few hundred years as we so casually think. The history lessons you were told in school have missed so very much. These lands have literally swarmed with people who lived, loved, and died for a multitude of same reasons you and I do. They toiled by the sweat of their brow. They hunted and killed with abandon, and drank deep and did dwell upon their creations.

And as with all peoples, there are good and bad and each may likely haunt our backyard. The bad have their way of lingering and reinforcing and magnifying their negativity and the good and innocent were perhaps horribly wronged an cannot yet deal with their powerful emotions – all of it binding the individual to this time and space, even if they seem to dance through it at times.

So, I had to go and see these ruins I've been reading of for myself, I had to feel the land, touch it, smell it, breathe it, and taste it. There was no other way for to understand what had happened here and why it was a forgotten unknown nexus for the paranormal, the strange, and the very obtuse. How had so many of these things slipped under the radar of all the other talented historians and researchers? How could they have all missed this?

I had to find out.

I drove down I-15 past St. George, through the Virgin River Gorge where Black Jack and his gang ambushed a ghost, through the corner of Arizona, through Mesquite and hung a left toward what remained of St. Thomas.

Bleached remains upon the desert floor like a cursed and blasted Sodom and Gomorrah. Remains that are all but forgotten. Skeletons of the lost west, a west that once was but is now slipping away into oblivion.

I walked the hills and valley floor, trotting up the trail next to poisonous springs beside sacred palms. I looked at jagged cliff faces searching for any sign of the thunderbirds of old.

If they remain, they sleep well yet.

Ghosts still haunt the cemetery here, the ghosts of everyone who ever left their loved ones behind, ghosts of every regret and trial, ghosts of every tragedy and triumph.

I went down to waters of Lake Mead and touched that shore, feeling what it might have been like to drown in that doorway to another world. How many spirits found themselves under those waves, forgotten all the more?

Today only foundations remain of some few more recent edifices. These are sad and lonely and lose all grandeur of that struggle that has gone on before.

I went to the Lost City to see what remained of that too and was melancholy at its tourist state. Rebuilt, removed and regurgitated it lacks everything the Toad told me it once was.

The Toad, yes I found him in that bag of documents, or did he find me?

He told me all about the majesty of what once was, of Coriantumr and foes. I can hear his whispers now, the glories of that Wicked Kingdom where the sons of Akish once ruled now the scorpions do impose. It stretched across the desert, blooming scarlet across its shadowy empire. The holy towers and vistas of an altered state ruled with iron and steel, gold littered the throne rooms of those secret robber kings while jewels set in silver rings danced upon their ladies wings, I saw how the mighty had fallen beneath their knighted step and broke all the . . .

Wait.

I heard nothing. I've been in the sun too long. A batrachian stone can't have told me anything, that's impossible, my imagination has run away with itself. Back to my typing, back to reality.

But the whispers, the whispers, they keep calling me . . .

"When the going gets weird, the weird turn pro."
— Hunter S. Thompson

Afterword:

The original Latin meaning of "anthology" is "a collection or gathering of flowers". A bouquet of the flowers of verse. Today when we think of anthology it is a compilation of stories that are supposed to be an assemblage of the beautiful flowering of literary prose.

I can't say that what I gave you here is anything more than a gathering of dead and desiccated roses but I hope it accents your library well.

Putting this project together was a labor of love, a sweaty, sleepless, frustrating, push me to the edge of my patience— yet also a needed labor of love and ego. I've never enjoyed putting something together quite as much as I have this and it is curious to me how much some these tales came together so quickly when I had no idea where on earth they were coming from, hence that very haunting mystique that leers over them like some specter of another world. That The Muse brought them to me is as much a mystery to me as anyone.

Perhaps it was the Toad.

Perhaps not.

"God never labels his gifts; He just puts them into our hands."
— M. R. James

Acknowledgments:

Thanks as always to my loving wife Melissa for her encouragement and ready ear. I could not have put this collection together near so well without her strength, guidance and patience.

Thank you to my children for their enthusiasm and attentiveness, they were among the first to hear these truly weird tales.

Thanks to Nathan Shumate for his wondrous work with the cover etc, always a talented man, please visit him at: http://nathanshumate.com/

Thanks to the Space Balrogs for their encouragement and friendship. Please visit their page as well. http://spacebalrogs.com/

Thank you to my friends and readers for giving this a chance.

Thanks to both my educational and spiritual inspirations, only one of you are still alive! Robert E. Howard, M.R. James, George W. Brimhall, Aaron James MacArthur, Sir Arthur Conan Doyle, J. Sheridan LeFanu, Edgar Allen Poe, Rudyard Kipling, Robert Nathan, Clark Ashton Smith, H.P. Lovecraft, Louis L'Amour, Bram Stoker, & Karl Edward Wagner.

About the Author:

David J. West is the bestselling author of *Heroes of the Fallen, Weird Tales of Horror,* and *The Mad Song.* He has an affinity for history, action-adventure, fantasy, westerns and pulp fiction horror blended with a sharp knife and served in a dirty glass—he writes what he knows.

He received first place when he was seven for writing a short story about a pack of wolves that outsmarted and devoured a hunter and his dog. Some children and parents may have been traumatized. He has never looked back.

His writing has since been praised in Meridian Magazine, Timpanogos Times, Hell Notes, and Amazing Stories Magazine which said his writing was "a solid collection of weird fiction." David's short stories have been published in the Lovecraft eZine, UGEEK, Sword & Sorcery Magazine, Iron Bound, Monsters & Mormons, Artifacts & Relics, Space Eldritch 1 and 2, and many more.

Before becoming an award-winning poet, novelist, and songwriter he was vagabonding all over North America sampling native fauna for brunch. When he isn't writing he enjoys traveling and visiting ancient ruins with intent on finding their lost secrets or at the very least getting snake bit. He collects swords, fine art and has a library of some seven thousand books. He currently lives in Utah with his wife and children. You can connect with him at:

http://david-j-west.blogspot.com
https://twitter.com/David_JWest
http://david-j-west.tumblr.com

24983375R00124

Made in the USA
San Bernardino, CA
13 October 2015